SIM

MYSTERY

Simenon, Georges, 1903–

Maigret's revolver

85 01781

MAIGRET'S REVOLVER

GEORGES SIMENON
MAIGRET'S REVOLVER

Translated from the French by Nigel Ryan

A Helen and Kurt Wolff Book
Harcourt Brace Jovanovich, Publishers
San Diego   New York   London

LIBRARY OF CONGRESS CATALOGING IN PUBLICATION DATA

Simenon, Georges, 1903–
   Maigret's revolver.

   Translation of: Le revolver de Maigret.
   "A Helen and Kurt Wolff book."
   I. Title.
PQ2637.I53R4713   1984   843'.912   84-4634
ISBN 0-15-155562-1

Designed by Mark Likgalter

Printed in the United States of America

First American edition 1984

A B C D E

MAIGRET'S REVOLVER

1

WHEN, LATER ON, Maigret thought about that case, it would always be as of something a little abnormal, linked in his mind with those illnesses that don't break out openly, but begin with vague aches and pains, symptoms too mild to claim one's attention.

There was, to start with, no complaint to the Police Judiciaire, no emergency call, no anonymous information, but, to go as far back as possible, a banal telephone call from Mme Maigret.

The black marble clock on the office mantelpiece had stood at twenty to twelve; he saw again distinctly the angle of the hands on its face. The window had been wide open, for it was June, and, beneath the hot sun, Paris had taken on its summer smell.

"That you?"

His wife had recognized his voice, obviously, but she still asked if it really was he speaking, not in doubt, but merely because she had always been awkward on the telephone. On Boulevard Richard-Lenoir, too, the windows must have been open. Mme Maigret at that hour would have finished the bulk of her housework. It was unusual for her to call him.

"It's me."

"I wanted to ask if you expect to be back for lunch."

It was even more unusual for her to telephone to ask him that question. He had frowned, not worried, but in surprise.

"Why?"

"Oh, nothing. Or, rather, there's someone here waiting to see you."

"Who?"

"No one you know. It's nothing. Only, if you weren't coming back, I wasn't going to make him wait."

"A man?"

"A young man."

She had probably taken him into the living room, where they scarcely ever set foot. The telephone was in the dining room, which they normally used, and where they entertained their friends. It was there that Maigret had his pipes, his armchair, Mme Maigret her sewing machine. From the embarrassed way she spoke, he realized that she hadn't dared to close the door between the two rooms.

"Who is it?"

"I don't know."

"What does he want?"

"I don't know that either. It's personal."

He had attached no importance to the matter. If he did anything about it, it was only because his wife was uncomfortable, and also because she seemed to have taken the visitor under her protection.

2

"I expect to leave the office about noon," he said finally.

He had only one more person to see, a woman who had already been to see him three or four times about threatening letters some neighbor was sending her. He rang for the porter.

"Show her in."

He lighted his pipe, and leaned back in his chair, resigned.

"Well, Madame, you've had another letter?"

"Two, Superintendent. I've brought them with me. In one of them, as you'll see, she admits it was she who poisoned my cat, and declares that if I don't move, it will soon be my turn. . . ."

The hands crept slowly around the face of the clock. He had to make a show of taking the matter seriously. It lasted for a little under a quarter of an hour. Then, just as he was going to get his hat from the closet, there was a knock at the door.

"You busy?"

"You! What are you doing in Paris?"

It was Lourtie, once one of his inspectors, who had been assigned to the flying squad in Nice.

"Just on my way through. I felt like taking a look at the old place again and saying hello to you. Do we have time to drink a *pastis* at the Brasserie Dauphine?"

"A quick one."

He was fond of Lourtie, a big-boned, strapping fellow with a voice like a choir leader's. In the brasserie, where they stood at the bar, there were several other inspectors. They spoke of this and that. The taste of the *pastis* was exactly what was needed for a day like that. They drank one, then a second, a third.

"It's time I was getting along. I'm expected at home."

"Can I walk partway with you?"

They had crossed the Pont-Neuf together, Lourtie and he, then walked as far as Rue de Rivoli, where it had taken Maigret a good five minutes to find a taxi. It had been ten of one when he at last climbed the three flights on Boulevard Richard-Lenoir, and, as usual, the door of his apartment opened before he had time to take the key from his pocket.

Right away he had noticed his wife's uneasy manner. Speaking low, because of the open doors, he had asked:

"He's still waiting?"

"He's gone."

"You don't know what he wanted?"

"He didn't tell me."

But for something in Mme Maigret's manner, he would have shrugged his shoulders and muttered:

"Good riddance!"

But instead of going into the kitchen and serving lunch, she followed him into the dining room with the air of someone who has excuses to make.

"Did you go into the living room this morning?" she finally asked.

"Me? No. Why?"

Why in fact should he have gone into the living room, which he loathed, before going to the office?

"It seemed all right to me."

"Well?"

"Nothing. I was trying to remember. I looked in the drawer."

"What drawer?"

"The one where you keep your revolver from America."

Only then had he begun to suspect the truth. When he had spent several weeks in the United States at the in-

4

vitation of the FBI, there had been a great deal of talk about weapons. The Americans had presented him, on his departure, with a revolver of which they were very proud, a Smith & Wesson .45 Special, with short barrel and highly sensitive trigger mechanism. His name had been engraved on it.

To J.-J. Maigret
from his FBI friends

He had never used it. But only the day before, he had taken it out of its drawer to show to a friend, or, rather, a colleague, whom he had asked in for a liqueur after dinner.

"Why J.-J. Maigret?"

He had asked the same question himself when he had been presented with the gun at a cocktail party in his honor. The Americans, who seemed normally to have two Christian names, had found out his. The first two, luckily: Jules-Joseph. In fact, there was a third: Anthelme.

"You mean my revolver has disappeared?"

"I'm just going to explain."

Before letting her speak, he went into the living room, which still smelled of cigarette smoke, and glanced at the mantelpiece, where he remembered having put the gun the evening before. It was no longer there. Yet he was sure he had not put it away in its place.

"Who's responsible for this?"

"Sit down, first of all. Let me give you your meal, or the roast will be overdone. Don't be mad."

He was.

"I think it's a bit much when you let a stranger make his way in here and . . ."

She left the room, came back with a plate.

5

"If you had seen him . . ."

"What age?"

"Quite a young man. Nineteen? Twenty perhaps?"

"What did he want?"

"He rang the bell. I was in the kitchen. I thought it was the gas man. I went and opened the door. He asked me if this was where Superintendent Maigret lived. I gathered, from his manner, that he mistook me for the maid. He was nervous, frightened-looking."

"And you showed him into the living room?"

"Because he told me he simply had to see you to ask your advice. My advice was to go and see you at your office. It seems it was too private."

Maigret kept his peevish look, but began to feel like smiling. He pictured the panic-stricken young man, on whom Mme Maigret had at once taken pity.

"What sort of young man?"

"A very nice boy. I don't know how to put it. Not very well off, but from a good family. I'm sure he'd been crying. He took some cigarettes from his pocket and then immediately apologized. So I told him: 'You can smoke. I'm used to it.' Then I promised to telephone you to make sure you'd be coming back."

"The revolver was still on the mantelpiece?"

"I'm certain it was. I didn't notice it there at that moment, but I remember it was there when I did the dusting this morning about nine, and no one else has been in."

If she hadn't replaced the revolver in the drawer, it was, he knew, because she had never been able to get used to firearms. Knowing the weapon wasn't loaded made no difference; she wouldn't have touched it for anything in the world.

He pictured the scene. His wife going into the dining room, speaking to him in low tones on the telephone, then coming back to say:

"He'll be here in half an hour at the latest."

Maigret asked:

"You left him alone?"

"Well, I had to see to lunch."

"When did he leave?"

"That's just what I don't know. At one point I had to fry some onions, and I closed the kitchen door so the smell wouldn't escape. Then I went to the bedroom to tidy up. I thought he was there all the time. Perhaps he still was. I didn't want to disturb him by going into the living room. It was only just after half past twelve that I decided to go and ask him to be patient, and found he wasn't there any longer. Are you mad at me?"

Mad at her about what?

"What do you think it's all about? He looked so unlike a thief!"

He certainly wasn't one, either! How could a thief have guessed that on that particular morning there was a revolver on the mantelpiece in Maigret's living room?

"You look worried. Was the gun loaded?"

"No."

"Well then?"

The question was a stupid one. Anyone who takes the trouble to get hold of a revolver has more or less some intention of using it. Wiping his mouth, Maigret got up and had a look in the drawer, where he found the cartridges in their place. Before sitting down again he called his office.

"That you, Torrence? Would you get hold of the gunsmiths in town . . . Hello! The gunsmiths, yes . . . Ask them if anyone has been in to buy cartridges for a Smith & Wesson .45 Special. . . . What? . . . .45 Special . . . In case no one has been in yet, if anyone does come this afternoon or tomorrow, tell them to find an excuse to keep the customer there for a moment and warn the nearest police station. . . . Yes . . . That's all. . . . I'll be at the office as usual. . . ."

When he had arrived at the Quai des Orfèvres at about half past two, Torrence already had the answer. A young man had gone to a gunsmith's on Boulevard Bonne-Nouvelle. They had no ammunition of the caliber asked for and had sent the customer to Gastinne-Renette. The latter had sold him a box.

"Did the boy produce the gun?"

"No. He showed them a scrap of paper with the make and caliber written on it."

Maigret had had other things to attend to that afternoon. Toward five o'clock he had gone up to the laboratory. Jussieu had asked him:

"Are you going to the Pardons' this evening?"

"With a fish *brandade* for dinner!" Maigret had replied. "Pardon called me up the day before yesterday."

"Me, too. I don't think Dr. Paul can come."

There are, just like that, periods in the lives of families during which they see a lot of another family, and then lose sight of them for no reason.

For about a year, every month, the Maigrets had dined with the Pardons, or, "at the Doc's." It was Jussieu, the head of the Forensic Laboratory, who had one evening taken the Inspector around to Dr. Pardon's house, on Boulevard Voltaire.

"You'll see! He's a man you'll like. An able man besides, who could have become one of our biggest specialists. I should add, specialist in any field, since, after being on the staff at Val-de-Grâce and an assistant of Lebraz, he spent five years on the staff at Sainte-Anne."

"And now?"

"He's become a G.P., by choice, works twelve or fifteen hours a day without bothering to find out if his patients are going to be able to pay him, and most of the time forgets to send his bill. Apart from that, his one passion is cooking."

Two days later, Jussieu had called him.

"Do you like cassoulet?"

"Why?"

"Pardon has invited us for tomorrow. At his house, you have just one dish, a regional one, by choice, and he likes to know in advance if his guests like it."

"Cassoulet suits me."

Since then there had been other dinners, the one with *coq au vin*, the couscous one, the *sole dieppoise*, and others besides.

This time it was to be *brandade de morue*. By the way, who was it, again, Maigret was going to meet at the dinner? Pardon had called him the day before.

"You free the day after tomorrow? You like *brandade*? Are you for or against truffles?"

"For."

They had got into the habit of calling each other Maigret and Pardon, while the women called each other by their Christian names. The two couples were almost the same age. Jussieu was ten years younger. Dr. Paul, the police medical expert, who often joined them, was older.

"Tell me, Maigret, would it bore you to meet one of my former schoolmates?"

9

"Why should it bore me?"

"I don't know. To tell you the truth, I wouldn't have invited him if he hadn't asked me to give him an opportunity to meet you. Just now he came to see me in my office—he's one of my patients as well—and insisted on knowing definitely if you were coming."

At half past seven that evening, Mme Maigret, who had bedecked herself in a flowered dress and a pretty straw hat, finished putting on her white cotton gloves.

"You ready?"

"I'm coming."

"Still thinking about the young man?"

"Of course not."

What was nice, among other things, about these dinners, was that the Pardons lived only five minutes' walk away. One could see the sunlight reflected in the top-floor windows. The streets smelled of warm dust. Children were still playing outdoors, and families had brought their chairs out to the sidewalks.

"Don't walk too fast."

He always walked too fast for her.

"You're sure it was he who bought the cartridges?"

Since that morning, especially since he had told her about Gastinne-Renette, she had had a load on her mind.

"You don't think he's going to kill himself?"

"Suppose we talk about something else?"

"He was so nervous! The cigarette butts in the ashtray were all picked to pieces."

The air was warm, and Maigret walked with his hat in his hand, like people who go for Sunday walks. They reached Boulevard Voltaire and just before the square disappeared into the building where the Pardons lived.

They took the narrow elevator, which always made the same noise as it started off, and Mme Maigret gave her usual little start.

"Come in. My husband will be here in a few minutes. He's just been called out on an urgent case, but it's only up the street."

It was seldom that a whole dinner went by without the doctor being disturbed. He would say:

"Don't wait for me."

And often, in fact, they went home without seeing him again.

Jussieu was already there, alone in the living room, where there was a grand piano and embroidery work on all the furniture. Pardon came bursting in a few minutes later, and at once plunged into the kitchen.

"Lagrange not here yet?"

Pardon was a little man, rather stout, with a very large head and bulging eyes.

"Wait a minute and I'll give you something that'll really make you sit up."

At his home there was invariably a surprise, maybe an unusual wine, maybe a liqueur, or, as in this case, a *pineau* from the Charentes, which a vineyard owner in Jonzac had sent him.

"Not for me!" protested Mme Maigret, who became tipsy after one glass.

They talked on. Here, too, the windows were open, life idled past on the sidewalk, and the air was gilded, the light a little more opaque and reddish.

"I wonder what Lagrange is doing."

"Who is he?"

"A fellow I knew in the old days at the Lycée Henri IV. If I remember rightly, he must have left us about his

11

third year. He lived on Rue Cuvier at the time, opposite the Jardin des Plantes, and his father impressed me because he was a baron, or pretended to be. I lost track of him for a long time, more than twenty years, and only a few months ago I saw him coming into my office, after waiting his turn. I recognized him at once."

He looked at his watch, then the clock.

"What surprises me is that he made such a fuss about coming and now isn't here himself. If he isn't here in five minutes we'll start dinner."

He filled the glasses. Mme Maigret and Mme Pardon did not speak. Although Mme Pardon was thin and the Superintendent's wife plump, they both had the same self-effacing attitude toward their husbands. It was rare during dinner for either of them to open their mouths; it was not until afterward that the two of them retired into a corner to whisper. Mme Pardon had a very long nose, much too long. You had to get used to it. At first it was embarrassing to look her in the face. Was it because of this nose, which her schoolmates must have laughed at, that she was so humble and looked at her husband as though to thank him for having married her?

"I bet everyone here," Pardon was saying, "had a boy or a girl of the Lagrange type at school. Out of twenty boys, or thirty, it is rare for there not to be at least one who, by the age of thirteen, is already a fat lump with a baby face and great pink legs."

"In my class, it was me," ventured Mme Maigret.

And Pardon said, gallantly:

"With girls it adjusts itself. Indeed, those are often the ones who turn out to be the prettiest in the end. We used to call François Lagrange 'Baby Cadum,' and there must have been thousands of them in all the schools of France

12

given that nickname by their school friends at that time, when the streets were full of pictures of the monster baby in the advertisements."

"He hasn't changed?"

"The proportions are no longer the same, naturally. But he's still a great tub. Ah, well, let's eat!"

"Why not phone him?"

"He hasn't got a telephone."

"Does he live near here?"

"A few yards away, on Rue Popincourt. I wonder what he wants exactly. The other day, at my office, he came trailing in with a magazine with your photograph on the front. . . ."

Pardon looked at Maigret.

"I'm sorry, but I don't know how I happened to let it out that I knew you. I must have added that you were a friend.

" 'Is he really like people say?' Lagrange asked me.

"I said yes, that you were a man who . . ."

"Who what?"

"It doesn't matter. Anyway, I said what I thought while I was examining him. He's diabetic. He also had glandular troubles. He comes in twice a week, he's so overanxious about his health. On the next visit, he talked about you again, wanting to know if I saw you often, and I said that we dined together once a month. It was then that he insisted on being invited, which surprised me, because since we left the Henri IV I've only seen him in my office. Let's sit down to dinner. . . ."

The *brandade* was a masterpiece, and Pardon had served a dry wine from somewhere around Nice, which went miraculously with the fish. After talking about fat people, they talked about redheads.

13

"It's true there's a redhead in every class, too."

This steered the conversation to the theory of genes. They always ended up by talking medicine, and Mme Maigret knew this pleased her husband.

"Is he married?"

With the coffee, they had got back to Lagrange, goodness knows why. The blue of the sky, a deep velvety blue, had slowly prevailed over the red of the setting sun; but they had not put on the lights, and they could see, through the windows, the balcony railings printing in inky black their wrought-iron arabesques. From a distant street corner came the strains of an accordion, and a couple on a neighboring balcony were talking in low voices.

"He was, from what he told me, but his wife died a long time ago."

"What does he do?"

"Business. Pretty vague sort of business, probably. His card says 'Company Director' with an address on Rue Tronchet. I called the address one day, when I wanted to cancel an appointment, and was told the offices had ceased to exist years ago."

"Any children?"

"Two or three. A daughter certainly, if I remember correctly, and a son he wants to find a steady job for."

They went back to medicine. Jussieu, who had worked at Sainte-Anne, recounted memories of Charcot. Mme Pardon was knitting and explaining a complicated stitch to Mme Maigret. The lights were put on. There were several mosquitoes. It was eleven o'clock before Maigret got up.

They left Jussieu at the corner of the boulevard, where he caught the métro at Place Voltaire. Maigret felt a bit full on account of the *brandade*, and perhaps also the Midi wine.

His wife, who had taken his arm, which she seldom did except when they were going home in the evening, wanted to say something. How did he sense this? She hadn't opened her mouth, and yet he was waiting.

"What are you thinking about?" he finally grunted.

"You won't be annoyed?"

He shrugged his shoulders.

"I'm thinking about the young man this morning. I wonder if, when we get back, you could telephone to see *if there's been anything.*"

She used a roundabout way of expressing herself, but he understood. She meant: ". . . to see if he's committed suicide."

Oddly enough, this was not the idea Maigret had in mind of what might happen. It was only a feeling, without any solid basis. It was not, in his case, a suicide that he was thinking of. He felt vaguely uneasy, without wishing to seem so.

"How was he dressed?"

"I didn't pay much attention to his clothes. I seem to remember he was in something dark, probably navy blue."

"His hair?"

"Fair. Blond, rather."

"Thin?"

"Yes."

"Good-looking boy?"

"Quite. To my mind."

He would have sworn she was blushing.

"You know, I didn't look at him much! I remember more than anything else his hands, because he fiddled

15

nervously with the brim of his hat. He didn't dare sit down. I had to bring a chair to him. He seemed to be expecting me to turn him out."

Back at home Maigret called the municipal police, to which all emergency calls were put through.

"Maigret here. Anything to report?"

"Only some Bercy cases, sir."

This, on account of the Halle aux Vins on Quai de Bercy, meant drunks.

"Nothing else?"

"A free-for-all on Quai de Charenton. Wait. Yes. Late in the afternoon, a drowned woman was taken out of the Saint-Martin canal."

"Identified?"

"Yes. A prostitute."

"No suicides?"

This to please his wife, who was listening, hat in hand, at the bedroom door.

"No. Not so far. Shall I call you if there's anything new?"

He hesitated. It annoyed him to appear interested in the affair—above all, in front of his wife.

"If you would."

He was not called again that night. Mme Maigret woke him with his coffee, and the bedroom windows were already open. Workmen could be heard loading crates on a truck in front of the store opposite.

"You see, he hasn't killed himself!" he said, as though he were getting his revenge.

"Perhaps they don't know about it yet."

He reached the Quai des Orfèvres at nine o'clock, met his colleagues at the conference in the Chief Commissioner's office. Just routine matters. Paris was quiet.

They had the description of the murderer of the woman fished out of the canal. His arrest was only a question of time. Probably he would be found dead drunk in some bar before the end of the day.

Around eleven o'clock, Maigret was called to the telephone.

"Who is it?"

"Pardon."

At the other end of the line, he seemed hesitant.

"Excuse me for disturbing you at your office. Yesterday I spoke to you about Lagrange, who had asked if he might be allowed to come to our dinner party. This morning, on my rounds, I went by his place on Rue Popincourt. I went in on the off chance, thinking perhaps he wasn't well. . . . Hello! Are you there?"

"I'm listening."

"I wouldn't have called you except that, after you went, my wife told me about the young man."

"What young man?"

"The young man and the revolver. It seems Madame Maigret told my wife how, yesterday morning . . ."

"Yes. Well?"

"Lagrange would be furious if he knew I've gone and warned you. I found him in a curious state. First of all, he let me knock for several minutes at the door of his rooms without answering, and I began to be uneasy, since the concierge had told me he was in. Finally he came, in bare feet and shirt sleeves, disheveled-looking. He seemed relieved to see it was me.

" 'I'm sorry about last evening . . .' he said, going back to bed. 'I wasn't feeling well. I still don't feel well. Did you mention me to the Inspector?' "

"What did you reply?" asked Maigret.

17

"I don't remember. I took his pulse, his blood pressure. He was not a pretty sight. He looked like someone who's just had a shock. The place was in chaos. He hadn't eaten, or had any coffee. I asked him if he was alone, and that at once alarmed him.

" 'You're afraid I may have a heart attack, aren't you?'

" 'Of course not! I was only surprised . . .'

" 'What about?'

" 'Don't your children live here?'

" 'Only my younger son. My daughter left as soon as she was twenty-one. The older boy is married.'

" 'Does the younger one work?'

"Then he began to cry, and it was like a wretched great creature being deflated.

" 'I don't know,' he stammered. 'He isn't here. He hasn't come back.'

" 'Since when?'

" 'I don't know. I'm all alone. I'm going to die all alone. . . .'

" 'Where does your son work?'

" 'I don't even know if he does work. He doesn't tell me anything. He's gone. . . .' "

Maigret listened, his face serious.

"Is that all?"

"Pretty much. I tried to cheer him up. He was rather pathetic. Usually he goes around looking quite grand; at any rate, he still keeps up appearances. To see him in those shabby rooms, sick in a bed that hadn't been made for several days . . ."

"His son is in the habit of staying out all night?"

"Not so far as I could see. It would be a pure fluke, obviously, if it was the same young man as . . ."

"Yes."

"What do you make of it?"

"Nothing so far. Is the father really ill?"

"As I told you, he's had a severe shock. His heart's not too good. He's there, sweating in his bed, terrified that he's going to die. . . ."

"You were quite right to telephone me, Pardon."

"I was afraid you would laugh at me."

"I didn't know my wife had told yours the story of the revolver."

"Have I put my foot in it?"

"Not at all."

He called the porter.

"No one else for me?"

"No, sir. Apart from the loony."

"Send him in to Lucas."

A regular customer, this was, a harmless madman who came in once a week to offer his services to the police.

Maigret hesitated a moment longer. Mainly out of self-respect, in actual fact. This story, seen in a certain light, was rather absurd.

On the Quai, he nearly took one of the police cars, then, still slightly from shame, decided to go to Rue Popincourt by taxi. It was less official. That way, there would be no one to laugh at him.

2

THE LODGE, on the right of the archway, was like a hole in the wall, lighted all day by a yellowish bulb, which hung on the end of a wire. Practically the entire space was taken up with objects that looked as if they fit in place like a child's set of blocks: a stove, a very high bed covered by a red quilt, a round table covered with oil-cloth, an armchair with a big ginger cat in it.

The concierge didn't open the door, but watched Maigret through the glass. When he didn't go away, she resigned herself to opening the pane. Her head was then framed in the window like an enlarged photograph, a bad enlargement, with blemishes, a bit faded, which might have been done at a fair. The black hair looked dyed, the rest was without color or shape. She waited. He said:

"Monsieur Lagrange, please?"

She did not reply at once, and he might well have thought her deaf. Finally she uttered, in a voice of hopeless boredom:

"Third on the left the far side of the courtyard."

"Is he in?"

It was not boredom, but indifference, perhaps contempt, perhaps even hatred for all that existed outside her aquarium. Her voice droned.

"Because the doctor came to see him this morning, he's probably in."

"No one went up after Doctor Pardon?"

Mentioning the name gave the impression he knew all about it.

"He wanted me to go up."

"Who?"

"The doctor. He wanted to give me a little money to go and clean the place up and get him something to eat."

"Did you go?"

She shook her head, without explaining.

"Why?"

She shrugged her shoulders.

"You don't get on with Monsieur Lagrange?"

"I've only been here two months."

"Does the last concierge still live around here?"

"She's dead."

It was useless, he knew, to try to get any more out of her. The entire establishment, the six-story building that faced the street, and the three-story building on the far side of the courtyard, with its tenants, its workers, its children, its comings and goings—all this represented, for her, the enemy, whose sole object in life was to disturb her peace.

As one emerged from the dark, cold archway, the courtyard seemed almost gay; it even showed a bit of grass struggling up between the flagstones. The sun was shining full on the yellowish plastered house front at the far end, a carpenter in his workshop was sawing pleasant-smelling wood, and in a carriage a child was sleeping, its mother looking down from time to time from a second-floor window.

Maigret knew the district, which was near his own; there were many houses like this in it. In the courtyard on Boulevard Richard-Lenoir, too, there was still a washroom without a seat, with a door that was always half open, as in a country yard.

He climbed the stairs slowly, pressed an electric bell, and heard it ring in the room. Like Pardon, he had to wait. Like him, too, he eventually heard light sounds, the slithering of bare feet on the floor, a cautious approach, and finally, he could have sworn, labored breathing near him on the other side of the latch. The door did not open. He rang again. Nothing moved this time, and, bending down, he could see the gleam of an eye at the keyhole.

He coughed, wondering whether he ought to give his name. Then, just as he was going to open his mouth, a voice said:

"One moment, please."

More steps, comings and goings, finally the click of the lock, the noise of a bolt. In the half-open doorway a tall man in a bathrobe was surveying him.

"Did Pardon tell you . . . ?" he stammered.

The bathrobe was old, worn out, the slippers, too. The man was unshaven, and his hair was disheveled.

"I am Superintendent Maigret."

A nod gave him to understand that he had been recognized.

"Come in! I am sorry about . . ."

He did not specify what. They went right into an untidy living room, where Lagrange hesitated, and Maigret, pointing to the open door of a bedroom, said:

"Do go back to bed."

"Thank you."

Sunshine flooded the cheap rooms, which did not look the way such rooms usually did, but more like a sort of camping place, though it would not be possible to say exactly why.

"I'm sorry . . ." the man repeated as he slipped into the unmade bed.

He was breathing with difficulty. His face glistened with sweat, and his big eyes didn't know where to rest. Underneath, Maigret was not much more at ease himself.

"Take the chair, here."

Seeing there was a pair of trousers on it, Lagrange repeated again:

"Sorry."

The Superintendent didn't know where to put the trousers; finally he left them on the foot of the bed and began, steadying his voice:

"Doctor Pardon told us yesterday we would have the pleasure of meeting you. . . ."

"I hoped so, yes. . . ."

"Were you in bed?"

He saw that the man was hesitating.

"In bed, yes."

"When did you begin to feel ill?"

"I don't know. Yesterday."

"Yesterday morning?"

"Maybe . . ."

"Heart?"

"And everything else . . . Pardon has been looking after me a long time. . . . Heart as well . . ."

"You're worried about your son?"

The man was looking at him just the way the big schoolboy he had once been must have looked at his teacher when he didn't know what to reply.

"He hasn't come back home?"

Another moment's hesitation.

"No . . . Not yet . . ."

"You wanted to see me?"

Maigret tried to affect the indifferent tones of a visitor. Lagrange, for his part, sketched a vague polite smile.

"Yes, I'd said to Pardon . . ."

"Because of your son?"

He looked suddenly astonished, repeated:

"My son?"

Then right away he shook his head.

"No . . . I didn't know then. . . ."

"You didn't know he was going away?"

Lagrange corrected him, as though the words were too emphatic:

"He hasn't been back."

"For how long? Several days?"

"No."

"Since yesterday morning?"

"Yes."

"You had a quarrel?"

Lagrange was in torment, but Maigret was determined to get to the bottom of it.

"In Alain's case, we've never quarreled."

24

He said this with a kind of pride, which didn't escape the Superintendent.

"And with your other children?"

"They don't live here any more."

"Before they left you?"

"That wasn't the same."

"I suppose you'd be glad if we found your son?"

Fear showed, once again.

"What do you intend to do?" the man asked.

He had bouts of energy, which made him seem almost like a normal person, then all of a sudden he would collapse, deflated, on his bed.

"No. You mustn't. I think it's better not to. . . ."

"You're worried?"

"I don't know."

"You're afraid of dying?"

"I'm ill. I've no strength left. I . . ."

He put his hand to his heart, and seemed to be feeling its beats anxiously.

"You know where your son worked?"

"Not recently. I didn't mean the doctor to talk to you about it."

"Yet two days ago you insisted on his arranging for you an interview with me."

"I insisted?"

"You wanted to see me about something, didn't you?"

"I was interested in seeing you."

"Nothing else?"

"I'm sorry."

It was the fifth time at least he had uttered those words.

"I'm ill, very ill. There's nothing else."

"However, your son has disappeared."

25

Lagrange became impatient.

"Perhaps he has simply done the same as his sister."

"What did his sister do?"

"When she was twenty-one, the very day of her coming of age, she left without a word, with all her belongings."

"A man?"

"No. She works in a lingerie shop, in the Champs-Elysées Arcade, and lives with a girlfriend."

"Why?"

"I don't know."

"You have another son, older?"

"Philippe, yes. He's married."

"You don't think Alain's gone to him?"

"They don't see each other. It's nothing, I tell you. Except that I'm ill, and I'm left all alone. I'm ashamed you've been disturbed. Pardon shouldn't have done it. I wonder why I told him about Alain. I suppose I was in a fever. Perhaps I still am. You mustn't stay here. It's all in a mess, and it must smell. I can't even offer you a drink."

"You haven't a cleaning woman?"

"She hasn't come."

It was obvious that Lagrange was lying.

Maigret didn't like to ask if he had any money. It was very hot in the bedroom, a stagnant heat, and a disagreeable odor hung in the air.

"You don't want me to open the window?"

"No. There's too much noise. I have a headache. I ache all over."

"Perhaps you'd better be taken to a hospital?"

The word frightened him.

"Above all, not that! I want to stay here."

"To wait for your son?"

"I don't know."

It was strange. At one moment Maigret was moved to pity, and then immediately afterward he was irritated, feeling that it was playacting. Perhaps the man was ill, but not, it seemed to him, to the point of collapsing on his bed like a slug, not enough to have tears in his eyes and lips quivering like a baby about to cry.

"Tell me, Lagrange . . ."

As he broke off, he caught a sudden firmer look, one of those sharp looks that women in particular dart furtively at you when they think they have been found out.

"What?"

"You're sure that when you asked Pardon to invite you to meet me you had nothing to tell me?"

"I swear I just said that offhand. . . ."

He was lying; that was why he found it necessary to swear. Again, just like a woman.

"You have no information to give me that would enable us to find your son?"

There was a chest of drawers in one corner, and Maigret, who had risen, went over to it, all the time conscious of the other man's eyes fixed on him.

"I'm going to ask you, just the same, to let me have a photograph of him."

Lagrange was about to reply that he didn't have one. Maigret was so sure of this that, with an almost mechanical gesture, he opened one of the drawers.

"Is it here?"

Everything was to be found there: keys, an old wallet, a cardboard box containing buttons, jumbled papers, gas and electric bills.

"Give it to me."

"What?"

"The wallet."

Afraid the Superintendent would examine the contents himself, he found the strength to raise himself on one elbow.

"Give it here. . . . I think I have a picture taken last year. . . ."

He was becoming feverish. His big pudgy fingers were trembling. From a small fold, where he knew it was, he pulled out a photograph.

"Since you insist. I'm sure there's nothing to it. You mustn't publish it in the papers. You mustn't do anything."

"I'll bring it back to you this evening or tomorrow."

This frightened him again.

"There's no hurry."

"What are you going to eat?"

"I'm not hungry. I don't need anything."

"And this evening?"

"I'll probably be better and able to go out."

"And if you aren't better?"

He was on the verge of sobbing with agitation and impatience, and Maigret was not so cruel as to impose himself any longer.

"Just one question. Where has your son Alain been working recently?"

"I don't know the name. . . . It was in an office on Rue Réaumur."

"What sort of office?"

"Advertising . . . Yes . . . it must have been an advertising office. . . ."

He made as if to get up and show his visitor out.

"Don't disturb yourself. Good-bye, Monsieur Lagrange."

"Good-bye, Superintendent. Don't hold it against me. . . ."

Maigret all but asked: "What?"

But what was the use? He remained standing a moment on the landing, to relight his pipe, and he could hear the bare feet on the floor, then the key in the lock, the bolt, and probably, also, a sigh of relief.

Passing in front of the lodge he saw the concierge's head in its frame, hesitated, stopped.

"You'd better go up from time to time, as Doctor Pardon advised, to see if he needs anything. He really is ill."

"He wasn't last night, when I thought he was making a moonlight getaway."

This had hung by a thread. Maigret, who had been on the point of going off, frowned, turned back.

"He went out last night?"

"He was fit enough to carry his big trunk, with the aid of a taxi driver."

"You spoke to him?"

"No."

"What time was it?"

"About ten o'clock. I hoped the rooms were going to be empty!"

"You heard him come back?"

She shrugged.

"Of course, since he's up there."

"With his trunk?"

"No."

Maigret was too near home to take a taxi. As he passed by a café, he remembered the *pastis* of the day before, which suited the early summer so well, and he had one at the bar, gazing, without seeing them, at some workmen in white overalls having drinks next to him.

As he crossed his own boulevard, he lifted his head and saw Mme Maigret passing back and forth· in the apartment, with the windows open. She must have seen him, too. At any rate, she recognized his footsteps on the stairway, for the door opened.

"Still nothing happened to him?"

She was again thinking of her young man of the day before and her husband took the photograph from his pocket, showed it to her.

"Is that him?"

"How did you get it?"

"It's him?"

"Certainly it's him! Is he . . . ?"

She must already have been imagining him dead and was upset about it.

"No, no. He's still alive and kicking. I've just come from his father."

"The one the doctor told you about yesterday?"

"Lagrange, yes."

"What did he say?"

"Nothing."

"So you still don't know why he took your revolver?"

"To use it, presumably."

He telephoned the Police Judiciaire, but nothing had happened that could be put down to Alain Lagrange. He ate a quick lunch, took a taxi to the Quai, went straight up to the photographic section.

"Print me enough copies of this for all the police in Paris."

He nearly changed his mind and had the picture circulated all over France, but wouldn't that have attached too much importance to the affair? What annoyed him was that ultimately the only real fact was that someone had taken his gun.

A little later on he called Lucas into his office. He had taken off his vest, and was smoking his enormous pipe.

"I'd like you to get hold of the taxis that work at night around Rue Popincourt. There's a stand on Place Voltaire. That must be the one. At this time, the night drivers are generally at home."

"What do I ask them?"

"If one of them, last night about ten o'clock, took a big trunk from a building on Rue Popincourt. I would like to know where he delivered it."

"That all?"

"Also ask if he took his fare back to Rue Popincourt."

"Right, Chief."

Already, at three o'clock, the radio cars were in possession of the photograph of Alain Lagrange; at four, it reached the police stations and posts with the caption: "*Warning! Armed!*" By six o'clock all the police in Paris going out on their beats would have it in their pockets.

As for Maigret, he was not too sure what to do. Embarrassment prevented him from taking the affair too seriously, and at the same time he felt uncomfortable in his office. He felt he was wasting time and ought to be doing something.

He would have liked a long conversation with Pardon about the Lagranges, but at that time the doctor's waiting room would be full of sick people. The idea of interrupting the consultations disconcerted him. He didn't even know what questions he would have asked.

He thumbed through the telephone directory, found

three advertising agencies on Rue Réaumur, and jotted them down almost mechanically in his notebook.

"Anything for me, Chief?" Torrence came in and asked a little later on.

But for that he wouldn't have given him the agencies to do.

"Telephone all three and find out which of them employed a young man named Alain Lagrange. If you find him, go over and get all the information you can. Not so much from the employers, who never know anything, as from the rest of the staff."

He lingered another half hour in his office, finishing odd jobs of no importance. Then he saw a curate who complained that money had been stolen from the poor boxes in his church. To receive the priest, he had put his jacket on. Alone once more, he in turn went out, took one of the police cars waiting on the Quai.

"The Champs-Elysées Arcade."

The sidewalks were overflowing with people. At the entrance to the Arcade there were more tourists, speaking every language, than there were Frenchmen. He didn't often go there, and was surprised to note that in a stretch of less than a hundred yards there were five women's lingerie shops. It embarrassed him to have to go in. He felt the salesgirls were looking at him ironically.

"You haven't a young lady by the name of Lagrange here, have you?"

"Is it something private?"

"Yes . . . that's to say . . ."

"We have a Lajaunie, Berthe Lajaunie, but she's on vacation. . . ."

At the third shop a pretty girl lifted her head sharply and said, already on the defensive:

"That's me. What do you want?"

She did not look like her father; perhaps like her brother Alain, with a very different expression, and, without knowing why, Maigret felt sorry for the man who fell in love with her. At first sight, indeed, she was charming, especially when she put on her salesgirl's smile. But behind the charm, he guessed that she was hard, exceptionally self-possessed.

"Have you seen your brother recently?"

"Why do you ask that?"

She glanced toward the back of the shop, where the manager was in a fitting room with a customer. Rather than talk in a void, Maigret preferred to show his badge.

"Has he done something wrong?" she asked in a low voice.

"It is Alain you're thinking of?"

"Who told you I work here?"

"Your father."

She didn't stop to think for long.

"If you really have to talk to me, wait for me somewhere in half an hour's time."

"I'll wait for you on the terrace of the café Le Français."

She watched him go without moving, her brows puckered, and Maigret spent thirty-five minutes watching the crowd flowing past, and moving his legs out of the way every time a waiter or passers-by knocked against them. She arrived, dressed in a light outfit, looking determined. He was sure she would come. She was not the girl to leave him in the lurch, or, once there, to show embarrassment. She sat in the chair he had kept for her.

"What will you have?"

"A port."

She arranged the hair on each side of her white straw toque, crossed her well-shaped legs.

"You know your father's ill?"

"He always has been."

There was no pity, no emotion in her voice.

"He's in bed."

"Very likely."

"Your brother's disappeared."

He saw that she was startled, that this piece of news surprised her more than she was willing to admit.

"That doesn't astonish you?"

"Nothing astonishes me."

"Why?"

"Because I've seen too much. What exactly do you want from me?"

It was difficult to reply point-blank to such a straight question, and she calmly took a cigarette from a case and asked:

"Do you have a light?"

He struck a match for her.

"I'm waiting."

"How old are you?"

"I presume it wasn't just to find out my age that you took all this trouble. According to your badge, you aren't a plain inspector, but a superintendent. In other words, someone important."

Examining him more closely:

"You're not the famous Maigret?"

"I'm Superintendent Maigret, yes."

"Has Alain killed someone?"

"Why do you think that?"

"Because for you to be on a case I imagine it must be serious."

34

"Your brother could be the victim."

"Has he really been killed?"

Still no emotion. True, she didn't seem to believe it.

"He's wandering around Paris somewhere with a loaded gun in his pocket."

"There must be other people doing that."

"He stole the revolver yesterday morning."

"Where?"

"From where I live."

"He went to your home? To your apartment?"

"Yes."

"When there was no one there? You mean he robbed you?"

This amused her. There was a sudden look of irony on her face.

"You're no more fond of Alain than of your father, are you?"

"I'm not fond of anybody, not even myself."

"How old are you?"

"Twenty-one and seven months."

"So it's seven months since you left your father's home?"

"You call that a home? Have you been there?"

"Do you think your brother is capable of killing someone?"

Wasn't it to make herself interesting that she replied, as if to rile him:

"Why not? Everyone is capable of it."

Anywhere but on this terrace, where a couple next to them were beginning to eavesdrop, he would probably have shaken her, so much did she exasperate him.

"Did you know your mother, mademoiselle?"

"Hardly—I was three when she died, immediately after Alain's birth."

35

"Who were you brought up by?"

"My father."

"He looked after his three children by himself?"

"When he had to."

"Which means what?"

"When he didn't have the money to pay for a maid. There was a time when we had two of them, but that didn't last. Sometimes it was a cleaning woman who looked after us, sometimes a neighbor. You don't give the impression of knowing the family very well."

"Have you always lived on Rue Popincourt?"

"We've lived everywhere, even near the Bois de Boulogne. We went up, we went down, then up again a little bit, before finally going downhill for good. Well, if you haven't anything more important to tell me, it's time I was getting along, because I have a date with my friend."

"Where do you live?"

"A few yards away, on Rue de Berri."

"At the hotel?"

"No. We've got two rooms in a private house. I suppose you want to know the number?"

She gave it to him.

"Anyway, it's been interesting meeting you. One tends to get ideas into one's head about people."

He didn't dare ask her what idea she had formed about him, or, more particularly, what idea she now had. She was standing up, her suit showing off her figure, and some customers looked at her, then looked at Maigret, no doubt telling themselves he was in luck. He rose in turn and left her in the middle of the sidewalk.

"I'm much obliged to you," he said grudgingly.

"Not at all. Don't worry too much about Alain."

36

"Why not?"

She shrugged her shoulders.

"An idea, that's all. I've a feeling that even though you may be the great Maigret, you've still got a lot to learn."

Thereupon she set off hurriedly in the direction of nearby Rue de Berri, and did not look back. He had not kept the police car. He took the métro, which was packed, and gave him an opportunity of venting his ill humor. He wasn't pleased with anyone, including himself. If he had met Pardon, he would have upbraided him for telling him about this Lagrange, who looked like a great ghost puffed up with wind, and he nursed a grievance against his wife for the revolver business, for which he wasn't far from holding her responsible.

All this was no concern of his. The métro smelled of laundry. The advertisements, always the same in the stations, nauseated him. Outside he found the sun almost burning, and he bore a grudge against the sun, too, for making him sweat. Seeing him go by, the porter realized he was in a bad mood and confined himself to a discreet nod.

On his desk, well in evidence, protected against gusts of wind by one of his pipes, which served for the occasion as a paperweight, there was a note:

"Please telephone the Station Police at Gare du Nord as soon as possible."

It was signed: *"Lucas."*

He picked up the telephone, asked for the number, with his hat still on, and, in order to light his pipe, held the receiver between his cheek and shoulder.

"Is Lucas still with you?"

Maigret had spent the grimmest two years of his life in

the Station Police office and he knew every aspect of it. He heard the voice of an inspector saying:

"For you. Your chief."

And Lucas:

"Hello! I wondered if you would be going back by the office. I telephoned your apartment as well."

"Did you find the driver?"

"A stroke of luck. He told me he was in a bar on Place Voltaire last evening, and a customer came and hunted him out, a great fat fellow, trying to look important, who had himself taken to Gare du Nord."

"To put a trunk in the checkroom?"

"That's right. You've got it. The trunk is still here."

"Have you opened it?"

"They won't let me."

"Who?"

"The station people. They insist on the ticket, or else a search warrant."

"Anything special?"

"Yes. It stinks!"

"You mean . . . ?"

"What you're thinking, yes. If it's not a stiff, the trunk is stuffed with rotten meat. Shall I wait?"

"I'll be there in half an hour."

Maigret made his way to the Chief Commissioner's office. The latter rang up the Public Prosecutor's office. The Public Prosecutor had already left, but one of his subordinates finally took the responsibility upon himself.

When Maigret came back through the duty room, Torrence had not returned. Janvier was dictating a report.

"Take someone with you. Go to Rue Popincourt and watch number 37B. There's a certain François Lagrange who lives on the third floor on the left at the far end of

38

the courtyard. Don't give yourselves away. He's big and fat, sickly looking. Take the son's picture with you, too."

"What do we do with him?"

"Nothing. If by any chance the son returns and goes out again, follow him carefully. He's armed. If the father goes out, which would surprise me, follow him, too."

Several minutes later Maigret was traveling in the direction of Gare du Nord. He recalled what the Lagrange girl had said to him at the café on the Champs-Elysées:

"Isn't everyone capable of it?"

Something like that, anyway. And now it was a question of murder. He threaded his way through the crowd, found Lucas chatting quietly with a Station Police inspector.

"You have the warrant, Chief? I may as well warn you right away that the guy in the checkroom is tough, and the police don't count for anything with him."

It was true. The man scrutinized the document, turned it over, turned it back, put on his glasses to examine the signature and the stamps.

"Seeing that I'm released from all responsibility . . ."

With a resigned but disapproving gesture he indicated a big gray trunk of old-fashioned design, its cloth torn in places, which had been tied up with rope. Lucas had exaggerated in saying it stank, but it gave out a stale smell that Maigret knew well.

"I hope you're not going to open it here."

It happened to be the rush hour. Crowds were pressing around the ticket windows.

"Is there someone who can help us?" Maigret asked the checkroom man.

"There are porters. You don't by any chance want me to lug it myself?"

The trunk would not fit into the small black police

39

car. Lucas had it loaded into a taxi. All this was not very regular. Maigret wanted to get it over with quickly.

"Where's it to go to, Chief?"

"The laboratory. That'll be best. Jussieu's probably still there."

He met Torrence on the stairs.

"You know, Chief . . ."

"You've found him?"

"Who?"

"The young man."

"No, but . . ."

"One minute then . . ."

Sure enough, Jussieu was upstairs. There were four or five of them around the trunk, photographing it from all sides and making various tests before opening it.

Half an hour later, Maigret called the Chief Commissioner's office.

"The Chief's just gone," someone replied.

He called him at his home, discovered he was dining that evening at a restaurant on the Left Bank. At the restaurant, he hadn't yet arrived. It meant another ten minutes' wait.

"I'm sorry to trouble you, Chief. It's Maigret, about the case I told you of. Lucas was right. I think you'd better come. It's someone important, and it may cause a sensation. . . ."

A second's pause.

"André Delteil, the Deputy . . . I'm sure of it, yes. . . . Right . . . I'll wait for you. . . ."

3

THE POLICE COMMISSIONER was attending a foreign-press dinner at a big hotel on Avenue Montaigne when the head of the Police Judiciaire succeeded in getting through to him on the telephone. At first he only let out an exclamation:

"M———!"

After which there was a silence.

"I trust the press isn't onto the case yet?" he finally murmured.

"Not so far. A reporter is hanging around in the corridor and realizes that something is going on. We won't be able to hide what it's all about for long."

The newsman, Gérard Lombras, an old hand at petty scandals, who made his little trip to the Quai des Orfèvres every evening, was sitting on the bottom step of the stairway just opposite the laboratory door, patiently smoking his pipe.

"Do nothing, say nothing, until I give the word," cautioned the Police Commissioner.

And, in his turn, from one of the booths, in the hotel, he called the Minister of the Interior. It was an evening of interrupted dinners, an exceptionally balmy evening, however, with languid strollers filling the streets of Paris. There were some on the quais as well, who must have wondered why, when night had not yet fallen, there were so many lighted offices in the old building of the Palais de Justice.

The Minister of the Interior, a native of Cantal who had kept his rough local accent and style of speech, exclaimed on hearing the news:

"Even dead, that fellow's a . . . nuisance!"

The Delteils lived in a big building on Boulevard Suchet, on the edge of the Bois de Boulogne. When, eventually, Maigret got permission to call, a manservant replied that Madame was not in Paris.

"You don't know when she'll be back?"

"Not before fall. She's in Miami. Monsieur is not here either."

Maigret asked on the off chance:

"Do you know where he is?"

"No."

"Was he in Paris yesterday?"

A moment's hesitation.

"I don't know."

"What do you mean?"

"Monsieur went out."

"When?"

"I don't know."

"The evening before last?"

"I think so, yes. Who is this?"

"Police Judiciaire."

"I don't know anything. Monsieur is not here."

"Does he have relatives in Paris?"

"His brother, Monsieur Pierre."

"You know his address?"

"I think he lives right near the Etoile. I can give you his telephone number. One minute . . . Balzac 51-02."

"You weren't surprised not to see Monsieur Delteil return?"

"No, sir."

"Had he warned you he wouldn't be coming back?"

"No, sir."

New figures began to fill the Forensic Laboratory. The Examining Magistrate, who had been sought out at the home of some friends where he had been playing bridge, had just arrived, as had the Public Prosecutor, and the two were conversing together in low tones. Paul, the police medical expert, who had also been dining out, was one of the last to appear, the perpetual cigarette between his lips.

"Shall I take him away?" he said, indicating the open trunk, where the corpse was still slumped.

"As soon as you've made your preliminary examination."

"I can tell you right away he's not fresh today. Good Lord! It's Delteil!"

"Yes."

A "yes" that spoke volumes. Ten years earlier, probably none of those who were present would have recognized the dead man. He was then a young lawyer more often to be met with at the Roland-Garros races or in the bars of the Champs-Elysées than at the Law Courts, and was more like a young movie star than a member of the bar.

A little later on he had married an American woman

43

with a private fortune, had installed himself on Boulevard Suchet, and three years afterward was a candidate in the general election. Even his opponents during the electoral campaign had not taken him seriously.

He had, nonetheless, been elected, by a narrow majority, and from the very next day had begun to get himself talked about. He did not, strictly speaking, belong to any party, but became the terror of them all, continually interrupting, exposing abuses, plots, intrigues, without anyone ever being able to see exactly what he was hoping to get out of it. At the beginning of each important session, ministers and deputies could be heard to ask:

"Is Delteil there?"

And brows would knit. If in fact he was there, bronzed like a Hollywood star, with his little brown mustache shaped like two commas, it meant there would be some fun.

Maigret had his peevish look. He had called the brother's number, a furnished home on Rue Ponthieu, where he had been advised to try Le Fouquet. Le Fouquet had put him on to Maxim's.

"Is Monsieur Delteil with you?"

"Who is calling?"

"Tell him it's about his brother."

He finally got him. They must have delivered his message incorrectly.

"That you, André?"

"No. This is the Police Judiciaire. Will you take a taxi and come around here?"

"I've got my car at the door. What's it all about?"

"Your brother."

"Has something happened to him?"

"Don't talk about anything until you've seen me."

"But . . ."

Maigret hung up, cast an irritated look at the groups forming in the vast room, then, since he wasn't needed right away, went down to his office. Lombras, the reporter, followed on his heels.

"You won't forget me, Superintendent?"

"No."

"In an hour it'll be too late for the next edition."

"I'll see you before then."

"Who is it? A big fish, isn't it?"

"Yes."

Torrence was waiting for him, but before speaking to him Maigret telephoned his wife.

"Don't expect me this evening, and more than likely not tonight at all."

"I thought as much when you didn't come home."

A silence. He knew what, or, rather, whom, she was thinking about.

"Is it him?"

"At any rate, he hasn't committed suicide."

"He's shot someone?"

"I just don't know anything."

He hadn't told them everything, upstairs. He didn't feel like telling them everything. He still had probably about an hour ahead of him of being bored by the bigwigs, after which he could take up his inquiry in peace once more.

He turned to Torrence.

"You've found the boy?"

"No. I saw his former employer and his colleagues. It's only three weeks ago that he left them."

"Why?"

"He got thrown out."

"In trouble?"

"No. It seems he's honest. But recently he was continually absent. At first they weren't bothered. Everyone rather took to him. Then, as he treated things more and more leisurely . . ."

"Did you find out anything about his habits?"

"Nothing."

"No girlfriend?"

"He never talked about his private affairs."

"No flirting with the typists?"

"One of them, not a pretty one, blushed when she mentioned him, but I got the impression he took no notice of her."

Maigret asked for a number on the telephone.

"Hello! Madame Pardon? Maigret here. Is your husband in? Tough day? Ask him to come to the phone for a second, would you?"

He wondered if, by any chance, the doctor had gone back, late in the day, to Rue Popincourt.

"Pardon? I'm very sorry to bother you. Have you got patients to see this evening? Listen. Things are getting serious in connection with your friend Lagrange. . . . Yes . . . I've seen him. . . . Something new has come up since I went to his place. I need your help. . . . That's right. . . . I would very much like you to come and pick me up here. . . ."

When he went upstairs again, still followed by Lombras, he caught sight of Pierre Delteil on the stairs, and recognized him from his likeness to his brother.

"Was it you who called me here?"

"Ssh! . . ."

He pointed to the reporter.

"Follow me."

He led him off upstairs, pushed the door closed just as Dr. Paul, who had been making a preliminary examination of the body, was straightening up.

"Recognize him?"

Everyone was silent. The scene was made more painful by the resemblance between the two men.

"Who did it?"

"It's your brother, all right?"

There were no tears, but clenched fists, set jaw, eyes that became fixed and hard.

"Who did it?" repeated Pierre Delteil, who was three or four years younger than the Deputy.

"We don't know yet."

Dr. Paul explained:

"The bullet entered through the left eye and lodged in the brain. It did not come out again. As far as I can judge, it's a small-caliber bullet."

On one of the telephones the Chief Commissioner was speaking to the Police Commissioner. When he came back to the group waiting for him, he passed on the instructions, which came from the Minister.

"A simple statement to the press, announcing that André Delteil, the Deputy, has been found dead in a trunk deposited in the checkroom at Gare du Nord. As few details as possible. There'll be time tomorrow."

Rateau, the Examining Magistrate, drew Maigret into a corner.

"You think it's a political crime?"

"No."

"An affair over a woman?"

"I don't know."

"You suspect someone?"

"I'll know tomorrow."

"I count on you to keep me posted. Phone me, even at night, if there's anything new. I'll be in my office tomorrow from nine o'clock in the morning onward."

Maigret vaguely nodded his assent, went and had a few words with Dr. Paul.

"All right, old man."

Paul went off to proceed with the autopsy. All this had taken time. It was ten o'clock at night when dark silhouettes merged into one another on the badly lighted stairway. The reporter did not leave the Superintendent's side.

"Come into my office a moment. You are right. It is a big fish. André Delteil, the Deputy, has been murdered."

"When?"

"We don't know yet. A bullet in the head. The body was found in a trunk deposited in the checkroom at Gare du Nord."

"Why was the trunk opened?"

The man had caught on right away.

"Nothing else for today."

"Have you got any clues?"

"Nothing else for today."

"Are you going to spend all night on the case?"

"Possibly."

"What if I followed you?"

"I would have you locked up on the first pretext at hand and leave you to cool off till tomorrow morning."

"I see."

"So that's settled."

Pardon knocked at the door, came in. The reporter asked:

"Who's this?"

"A friend."

"May we know his name?"

"No."

They were left alone together at last, and Maigret began by taking off his jacket and lighting a pipe.

"Sit down. Before going over there, I would like to have a little talk, and it's better for it to be here."

"Lagrange?"

"Yes. One question, to begin with. Is he really ill, and to what extent?"

"I was expecting that and I've been thinking about it all the way here, because it's not easy to answer categorically. Ill, yes, that's certain. He contracted diabetes some ten years ago."

"Which doesn't stop him leading a normal life?"

"Hardly at all. I gave him insulin. I've taught him to give himself his own injections. When he eats away from home, he always has a little folding scale in his pocket on which to weigh certain foods. With insulin, it's important."

"I know. Well?"

"Do you want a diagnosis in technical terms?"

"No."

"All his life he's suffered from glandular trouble, which is the case with most people of his physical type. He's soft, impressionable, easily depressed."

"And his present state?"

"It's here that it becomes trickier. I was very surprised this morning to find him in the state you saw him in. I examined him carefully. Although hypertrophied, the heart's not bad . . . no worse than it was a week or two ago, when Lagrange was going around as usual."

"You've considered the possibility of a hoax?"

Pardon had considered it, that could be seen from his expression. A scrupulous man, he was picking his words with care.

"I presume you have good reason to ask me that?"

"Grave reasons."

"His son?"

"I don't know. I'd better give you all the facts. Forty-eight hours ago, a man was killed, more than likely in the apartment on Rue Popincourt."

"Has he been identified?"

"It's Deputy Delteil."

"Did they know each other?"

"Our inquiries will tell us. The fact remains that last evening, while we were dining with you and talking about him, François Lagrange called a taxi to the front of his building and, with the help of the driver, brought down a trunk containing the corpse, to take it to Gare du Nord and deposit it. Does that surprise you?"

"It would be a surprise any time."

"You understand now why I am anxious to know if, when you examined him this morning, François Lagrange was ill to the extent he wanted people to believe, or if he was pretending."

Pardon rose.

"Before answering, I would like to examine him again. Where is he?"

He supposed that Lagrange had been brought to one of the offices of the Police Judiciaire.

"Still at home, in bed."

"Doesn't he know anything?"

"He doesn't know we've discovered the body."

"What are you going to do?"

"Go over there with you, if you're prepared to come with me. Do you like him?"

Pardon hesitated, then replied frankly:

"No!"

"Sympathy?"

"Let's say pity. I wasn't pleased to see him come into my office. Rather irritated, actually, as I always am in the presence of weaklings. But I can't forget that he has had to bring up his three children by himself, or that when he talked about his younger son, his voice trembled with emotion."

"Skin-deep sentimentality?"

"I wondered about that. I don't like men who weep."

"Did he ever cry in front of you?"

"Yes. Once in particular, when his daughter deserted him, without even leaving him her address."

"I've seen her."

"What does she have to say?"

"Nothing. She doesn't waste any tears! You coming with me?"

"I suppose it'll take some time?"

"Possibly."

"Mind if I give my wife a call?"

It was dark when they took their places in one of the police cars. All the way they were silent, each engrossed in his own thoughts, each, probably, also apprehensive of the scene they were about to face.

"Stop at the corner of the street," Maigret told the driver.

He recognized Janvier opposite 37B.

"A colleague of yours?"

"As a precaution I hid him in the courtyard of the building."

"The concierge?"

"She won't take any notice of us."

Maigret rang, made Pardon go in front of him. The

lodge was no longer lighted. The concierge didn't ask who they were, but the Superintendent thought he could make out the light blur of her face behind the window.

Above, on the third floor, there was a light in one of the rooms.

"Let's go up."

He knocked, failing to find the bell in the darkness because the stairwell lighting was not working. A shorter time elapsed than in the morning before a voice inquired:

"Who is it?"

"Superintendent Maigret."

"One moment please . . ."

Lagrange must have been putting on his bathrobe again. His hands were trembling, for he had trouble in turning the key in the lock.

"Have you found Alain?"

All of a sudden he saw the doctor in the semidarkness, and his face changed, turned still paler than usual. He stood there, without moving, no longer knowing what to do or say.

"May we come in?"

Maigret sniffed, recognized the smell that pervaded his nostrils, a smell of burned paper. Lagrange's beard had grown a bit more since the Superintendent's visit, and the bags under his eyes were more pronounced.

"Considering your state of health," Maigret began at last, "I didn't want to come without being accompanied by your doctor. Pardon has consented to take the trouble. I presume you have no objection to his examining you?"

"He listened to my chest this morning. He knows I'm ill."

"If you'll get back into bed, he'll examine you again."

Lagrange was on the point of protesting, as could be seen from his expression, but finally he resigned himself, went into the bedroom, removed his bathrobe, and lay down.

"Uncover your chest," Pardon said gently.

While he was being examined, the man stared fixedly at the ceiling. As for Maigret, he paced back and forth in the room. There was a chimney with a black damper, which he lifted, and behind the shutter he found some paper ashes which had been carefully reduced almost to powder with a poker.

From time to time Pardon muttered professional phrases.

"Turn over. . . . Breathe in. . . . Breathe deeper. Cough. . . ."

There was a door not far from the bed, and the Superintendent pushed it, found an unoccupied room, which must have belonged to one of the children, with an iron bedstead from which the mattress had been removed. He switched on the light. The room had become a sort of glory hole. A pile of weekly papers lay in one corner, with tattered books, including schoolbooks, a leather suitcase covered with dust. On the right, near the window, a patch of the floor the shape of the trunk found in Gare du Nord was a lighter color than the rest.

When Maigret came back into the adjoining room, Pardon was standing up, with a preoccupied look.

"Well?"

He did not reply at once, was avoiding Lagrange's eyes, which were fixed on him.

"In all conscience, I think he's in a fit state to reply to your questions."

"You hear, Lagrange?"

The man was looking from one to the other of them in silence, and his eyes were a wretched sight, like those of a wounded beast staring at the men bending over it and trying to understand.

"You know why I am here?"

Lagrange must have come to a decision, probably during the examination, because he remained silent, and not a muscle of his face moved.

"Why not admit you know very well, that you've been expecting it since this morning, and that it's fear which is making you ill?"

Pardon had gone to sit in a corner, one elbow over the back of his chair, chin in hand.

"We have discovered the trunk."

There was no shock. Nothing happened, and Maigret could not even have sworn that for the fraction of a second there had been an added intensity in those pupils.

"I'm not saying that you killed André Delteil. It's possible that you are innocent of the crime. I admit I don't know anything of what happened here, but I am certain it was you who took the corpse, shut up in your trunk, to the checkroom. In your own interest it would be better for you to speak."

Still no sound, no movement. Maigret turned to Pardon, at whom he shot a discouraged glance.

"I would even like to believe that you are ill, that the effort you made last evening and the emotional upset have shaken you. All the more reason to answer me frankly."

Lagrange closed his eyes, opened them again, but his lips did not part.

"Your son is on the run. If he did the killing, we won't

be long in getting our hands on him, and your silence doesn't help him at all. If it was not him, it's better, for his safety, that we should know. He's armed. The police are warned about it."

Maigret had approached the bed, had perhaps leaned over it a bit without realizing, and at last the man's lips moved; he stammered something.

"What did you say?"

Then, in a frightened voice, Lagrange cried out:

"Don't hit me! You've no right to hit me!"

"I have no intention of doing so, and you know it."

"Don't hit me. . . . Don't . . ."

And all of a sudden he threw back the covers, cringed, made as if to ward off an attack.

"I don't want . . . I don't want to be hit. . . ."

It was ugly to see. It was painful. Once more, Maigret turned to Pardon as if to seek his advice. But what advice could the doctor give him?

"Listen, Lagrange. You are perfectly lucid. You're no longer a child. You understand me extremely well. And a short while ago you weren't so ill, since you had the energy to burn some compromising papers. . . ."

A lull, as though the man were getting his breath, only to break out more violently than ever, to shout this time:

"Save me! . . . Help! . . . They're hitting me! . . . I don't want them to hit me! . . . Let me go!"

Maigret seized one of his wrists.

"That's enough of that, do you hear?"

"No! No! No!"

"Are you going to shut up?"

Pardon had risen, and then came over to the bed, looking intently at the sick man.

"I don't want . . . Leave me. . . . I'll wake the whole place up. . . . I'll tell them. . . ."

Pardon murmured in his ear:

"You won't get anything out of him."

Hardly had they moved away from the bed when Lagrange became motionless and relapsed into his silence.

The two of them held council in the corner.

"You think his mind is really deranged?"

"I can't be positive."

"It's a possibility?"

"It's always a possibility. He ought to be put under observation."

Lagrange had slightly moved his head so as not to lose sight of them, and it was evident that he was listening. He must have understood the last few words. He seemed pacified. Nevertheless, Maigret returned to the charge, not without weariness.

"Before you make any decision, Lagrange, I would like to warn you of one thing. I have an arrest warrant out in your name. Downstairs two of my men are waiting. Unless I get satisfactory replies to my questions, they are going to take you to the Police Infirmary."

No reaction. Lagrange was gazing at the ceiling with such a faraway look that one might have wondered whether he was listening.

"Doctor Pardon can assure you that there are almost infallible methods of exposing malingerers. You were not mad this morning. No more were you when you burned your papers. You aren't now, I feel sure."

Was there really a vague smile on the man's lips?

"I haven't struck you, and I'm not going to strike you. I'm just telling you again that the attitude you're adopt-

56

ing won't get you anywhere, and will only make people unsympathetic, if not worse. Have you made up your mind to answer?"

"I don't want them to hit me!" he repeated in a toneless voice, as if mumbling a prayer.

Maigret, with shoulders hunched, went and opened the window, leaned out, called to the inspector waiting in the yard.

"Come up with Janvier!"

He closed the window again and began pacing up and down the room. Footsteps were heard on the stairs.

"If you want to dress, you can. If not, they'll carry you as you are, wrapped in a blanket."

Lagrange merely went on moving his lips, repeating the same syllables, so that they ended up by meaning nothing at all.

"I don't want them to hit me. . . . I don't want them . . ."

"Come in, Janvier. . . . You, too . . . Just take him to the Infirmary. . . . No use dressing him, since he's quite capable of starting to struggle again . . . Just in case, put the handcuffs on him. . . . Wrap him in a blanket. . . ."

A door had opened on the floor above. A window was lighted on the other side of the courtyard, and they could see a woman leaning out of her window, and a man getting out of bed behind her.

"I don't want them to hit me! . . ."

Maigret didn't look, heard the click of the handcuffs, then heavy breathing, footsteps, bumps.

"I don't want them to . . . I . . . Help! . . . Save me!"

One of the men must have put a hand over his mouth, or gagged him, for the voice became fainter, then ceased; the footsteps reached the staircase.

The silence, immediately afterward, was uncomfortable. The Superintendent's first move was to light his pipe. Then he looked at the unmade bed, from which a sheet trailed out into the middle of the room. The old slippers were still there, the bathrobe on the floor.

"Your views, Pardon?"

"You'll have trouble."

"I'm sorry to have mixed you up in this case. It wasn't a pretty sight."

As though a detail had come back to him, the doctor muttered:

"He was always very frightened of dying."

"Ah!"

"Every week he used to complain of new illnesses, questioned me at length to find out if they were serious. He used to buy medical books. We ought to find them around somewhere."

Maigret in fact found them in the chest of drawers, and there were markers at certain pages.

"What are you going to do?"

"To start with, the Police Infirmary will see to him. As for me, I'm going on with the case. What I'd like more than anything would be to find his son."

"You've got an idea it's him?"

"No. If Alain had done the killing, he wouldn't have needed to steal my revolver. Actually, by the time he was at my house, the crime had already been committed. The death dates back forty-eight hours at least—to Tuesday, in fact."

"Are you staying here?"

"A few minutes. I'm waiting for the men I got Janvier to send. In an hour I'll have Doctor Paul's report."

It was Torrence who came a little later on, accom-

panied by two colleagues and some forensic and crim-
inal records men complete with cameras. Maigret gave
them instructions, while Pardon stood to one side, still
looking worried.

"You coming?"

"I'm with you."

"Can I drop you at home?"

"I would really like to ask your permission to go
around to the Police Infirmary. But perhaps my colleagues over there would take a dim view."

"On the contrary. Have you got an idea?"

"No. I would just like to see him again, perhaps try
once more. He's a difficult case."

It did them good to breathe the air in the streets once
again. The two men reached the Quai des Orfèvres, and
Maigret knew in advance that there would be more
lighted windows than usual.

Pierre Delteil's sports car was still parked there. The
Superintendent frowned. He found the reporter Lombras
on guard in the waiting room.

"The brother's waiting for you. Still nothing for me?"

"Still nothing, my boy."

He spoke without thinking, for Gérard Lombras was
almost his own age.

PIERRE DELTEIL was aggressive from the start. For example, while Maigret was giving instructions to little Lapointe, who had just come on duty, he stood by the desk, his buttocks resting on its edge, strumming the tips of his well-manicured fingers on a silver cigarette case. Then, when Maigret changed his mind just as Lapointe was going out, and asked him to order some sandwiches and beer, he deliberately twisted his lips into a sardonic smile.

True, he had received a serious shock, and since then his nervousness had continually increased, to a point where it became tiring to watch him.

"At last!" he cried when the door had closed and the Superintendent sat down at his desk.

And, because the latter was looking at him as though seeing him for the first time:

"I suppose you're going to decide on a vice crime or some affair with a woman? They must have given you instructions from above to hush up the business? Let me tell you this . . ."

"Sit down, Monsieur Delteil."

He would not sit down at once.

"I hate talking to a man standing up."

Maigret's voice was a bit weary, a bit hollow. The ceiling light was not on, and the desk lamp only diffused a green glow. Pierre Delteil finally settled himself in the chair that was offered him, crossed, then uncrossed his legs, opened his mouth to say something else disagreeable, but didn't have time to utter a word.

"Pure formality," Maigret interrupted him, reaching out a hand toward him without bothering to look at him. "Would you show me your identity card?"

He examined it with care, like a frontier policeman, turned it over and back again in his hands.

"Film producer," he read out finally, next to the heading "Profession." Have you produced many films, Monsieur Delteil?"

"The fact is that . . ."

"Have you produced one?"

"It's not yet in production, but . . ."

"If I understand you correctly, you haven't produced anything at all. You were at Maxim's when I got you on the telephone. A little while before, you were at Le Fouquet. You live in a furnished apartment in a pretty expensive building on Rue de Ponthieu and you own a magnificent car."

He now examined him from head to foot, as though to appraise the cut of the suit, the silk shirt, the shoes, which came from the best shoe manufacturer.

"You have private means, Monsieur Delteil?"

"I don't see the point of these . . ."

"These questions," the Superintendent finished, placidly. "None. What did you do before your brother became a deputy?"

"I worked on his election campaign."

"And before that?"

"I . . ."

"Just so. In short, for several years, you've more or less been your brother's gray eminence. In return, he provided for your needs."

"Are you trying to humiliate me? Is that part of the instructions you've received? Why not admit that those people know perfectly well it's a political crime and they've told you to suppress the truth at all costs. It's because I realized that, up there, that I waited for you. Let me inform you . . ."

"You know the murderer?"

"Not necessarily, but my brother was becoming a nuisance, and it had been arranged for . . ."

"You may light your cigarette."

This time there was no reply.

"I suppose, in your eyes, there is no solution other than a political crime?"

"Do you know the culprit?"

"Here, Monsieur Delteil, it's I who ask the questions. Had your brother any mistresses?"

"It's common knowledge. He made no secret of it."

"Not even from his wife?"

"He had still less reason to conceal it, because they were getting divorced. That's one of the reasons why Pat is now in the States."

"Is it she who's asking for the divorce?"

Pierre Delteil hesitated.

"For what reason?"

"Probably because she's got bored with it all."

"Your brother?"

"You know the Americans?"

"I've met one or two."

"Rich ones?"

"Some."

"In that case you must know that they marry as a sort of game. Eight years ago, Pat was passing through France. It was her first visit to Europe. She decided to stay, to have her own mansion in Paris, to live the life of Paris . . ."

"And to have a husband playing a part in that same Parisian life. Was it she who pushed your brother into politics?"

"He always had the idea of going into it."

"So he simply took advantage of the means that the marriage placed at his disposal. You mean that, fairly recently, his wife had enough of it and went back to the States to demand a divorce. What would have become of your brother?"

"He would have continued with his career."

"What about money? Usually, rich Americans take the precaution of marrying under a separate–maintenance arrangement."

"Nevertheless, André would never have accepted her money. Anyhow, I don't see where these questions . . ."

"Do you know this young man?"

Maigret handed him the photograph of Alain Lagrange.

Pierre Delteil looked at it uncomprehendingly, raised his head.

"Is that the murderer?"

"I'm asking if you've seen him before."

"Never."

"Do you know a man named Lagrange, François Lagrange?"

He began to search his memory, as though the name was not entirely unknown to him and he was trying to place it.

"I think, in certain circles," Maigret prompted him, "he is called 'Baron Lagrange.'"

"Now I know whom you're talking about. Most of the time people just say 'the Baron.'"

"You know him well?"

"I meet him from time to time at Le Fouquet or other places. I occasionally say hello. I must have drunk an apéritif with him. . . ."

"Did you have any business dealings?"

"Thank God, no."

"Your brother saw him often?"

"Same as me, probably. Everyone knows the Baron, more or less."

"What do you know about him?"

"Practically nothing. He's an idiot, a soft idiot, a great slob who tries to worm his way in."

"What's his profession?"

And Pierre Delteil, more naïvely than he would have wished:

"Does he have a profession?"

"I presume he must have means of support?"

Maigret almost added: "Not everyone's lucky enough to have a deputy for a brother."

He didn't do so because it was no longer necessary. Young Delteil was coming to heel, without noticing his own change of attitude.

"He's in some vague sort of business. At least, I suppose so. He isn't the only one in his position. He's the kind of man who buttonholes you and tells you he's just pulling off a deal involving several hundred million, and ends up by asking you to lend him the price of a dinner or a taxi."

"He must have got around to touching your brother?"

"He tried to touch everybody."

"You don't think your brother could have made use of him?"

"Certainly not."

"Why?"

"Because my brother distrusted idiots. I don't see what you're driving at. I get the feeling you know something you don't intend to tell me. What I still don't understand is how they knew that a trunk left in the checkroom at Gare du Nord contained André's body."

"They didn't know."

"It was just chance?"

He was beginning to sneer again.

"Almost sheer chance. One more question. What reason would a man like your brother have had to pay a visit, at his home, to a man like the Baron?"

"Did he pay him a visit?"

"You haven't answered me."

"It doesn't seem likely to me."

"A crime, at the start of the investigation, never seems likely."

Because there was someone knocking at the door, he called out:

"Come in!"

It was the waiter from the Brasserie Dauphine with the sandwiches and beer.

"Would you like some, Monsieur Delteil?"

65

"Thank you, but . . ."

"No, thank you?"

"I was just having dinner when . . ."

"I won't keep you any longer. I've got your telephone number. Maybe I'll need you tomorrow or the day after."

"In fact, you altogether discount the idea of a political crime?"

"I discount nothing. As you see, I'm working on it."

He picked up the telephone, to make quite clear that the interview was over.

"Hello! Is that you, Paul?"

Delteil hesitated, finally went to get his hat and made for the door.

"At any rate, you can be sure I won't let it rest. . . ."

Maigret waved a hand at him:

"Good night! Good night!"

The door closed once again.

"Maigret here . . . Well? . . . Yes, as I suspected . . . In your opinion he was killed on Tuesday evening, perhaps during the course of the night? . . . Does that tally? . . . Roughly speaking . . ."

It was on Tuesday, too, but in the afternoon, that François Lagrange had telephoned for the last time to the doctor to make sure that Maigret would be at the dinner the following day. At that time he still wanted to meet the Superintendent, and it was more than likely it was not out of mere curiosity. He couldn't then have been expecting the Deputy's visit, but perhaps he foresaw it for one of the next few days?

On Wednesday morning his son Alain appeared at Boulevard Richard-Lenoir, so nervous, looking so frightened, according to Mme Maigret, that she felt sorry for him and took him under her protection.

What did the young man go there for? To ask advice? Had he seen the murder? Had he discovered the body, which was probably not yet in the trunk?

The fact remained that the sight of Maigret's gun made him change his mind, that he took the weapon, left the apartment on tiptoe, and dashed into the first gun shop he came across to buy ammunition.

So he had some idea in his head.

The same evening, his father was not at the Pardons' dinner party. Instead, he got hold of a taxi driver and, with his help, went and deposited the body at Gare du Nord, after which he retired to bed and became ill.

"The bullet, Paul?"

As he expected, it had not been fired from his American revolver, since the weapon, at the time of the murder, was still at his home, but from a small-caliber gun, a 6.35, which would not have done much harm if the shot, hitting the left eye, had not entered the brain.

"Anything else to report? The stomach?"

The latter contained the remains of a copious dinner, and digestion had only just begun. That put the crime, according to Dr. Paul, at about eleven o'clock in the evening, Delteil, the Deputy, not being one of those who dine early.

"Thanks, old man. . . . No, the problems I've still got to solve aren't in your province."

He began to eat, all alone in his office, where there was still only a greenish light. He was uncomfortable, ill at ease. He found the beer tepid. He hadn't thought of ordering coffee, and, wiping his lips, he went and fetched the bottle of cognac he kept in his closet, and poured himself a glass.

"Hello! Get me the Police Infirmary."

He was surprised to hear Journe's voice. The professor had gone out of his way to answer himself.

"You've had time to look at my customer? What do you think of him?"

A definite answer would have eased his mind a bit, but old Journe was not the man for definite answers. He delivered, over the telephone, a lecture studded with technical terms, from which it emerged that there was about a sixty percent chance that Lagrange was a fraud, but that, short of a mistake on his part, weeks could pass before they had any scientific proof of it.

"Is Doctor Pardon still with you?"

"He's just about to leave."

"What's Lagrange doing?"

"Absolutely quiet. He let himself be put to bed and began talking to the nurse in a childish voice. He told her in tears that people had wanted to beat him, that everyone was set against him, that it had been like that all his life."

"Can I see him in the morning?"

"Whenever you like."

"I'd like a word with Pardon."

And, to the latter:

"Well?"

"Nothing new. I'm not altogether of the Professor's opinion, but he's more of an expert than I, and it's a long time since I gave up psychiatry."

"What's your personal opinion?"

"I'd rather have a few hours to think it over before saying. It's too serious a matter to give an opinion lightly. Aren't you going home to bed?"

"Not yet. I probably won't get any sleep tonight."

68

"You don't need me any more?"

"No, old man. Thanks very much. Apologize to your wife for me again."

"She's used to it."

"So's mine, fortunately."

Maigret rose, with the idea of going around to Rue Popincourt to see how his men were getting on. Because of the burned papers in the fireplace, he was not too hopeful that they'd find a clue, but he wanted to poke around in the corners of the rooms.

Just as he was getting his hat, the telephone rang.

"Hello! Superintendent Maigret? Faubourg Saint-Denis police station here. I was told to telephone you just in case. It's Lecoeur speaking."

The man was plainly very excited.

"It's about the young man in the photograph they sent us. I've got a character here . . ."

He corrected himself:

". . . person here who's just had his wallet stolen on Rue de Maubeuge . . ."

The victim must have been listening, causing Lecoeur to pick his words.

"It's a businessman from the provinces. . . . Hold on . . . From Clermont-Ferrand . . . He was going along Rue de Maubeuge, about half an hour ago, when a man came out of the darkness and brandished a large gun under his nose . . . a young man, to be more precise. . . ."

Lecoeur spoke to someone beside him.

"He says a very young man, almost a boy. . . . It seems his lips were trembling, so it was all he could do to say: 'Your wallet, please.' . . ."

Maigret frowned. Ninety-nine times out of a hundred an assailant simply says: "Your wallet!"

And in that alone could be recognized the amateur, the beginner.

"When the gentleman spoke about a young man," Lecoeur went on, not without a touch of self-satisfaction, "I at once thought of the picture issued to us yesterday, and I showed it to him. He recognized it without hesitating. . . . What? . . ."

It was the Clermont-Ferrand businessman talking, whose voice Maigret could hear stating emphatically:

"I'm absolutely certain of it!"

"What did he do then?" Maigret asked.

"Who?"

"The assailant."

Two voices again, as when a radio is not properly tuned in, two voices saying the same thing:

"He ran away."

"In which direction?"

"Boulevard de la Chapelle."

"How much money was there in the wallet?"

"About thirty thousand francs. What shall I do? You want to see him?"

"The man? No. Take down his statement. . . . One moment. Just put him on the line."

The man immediately said:

"My name is Grimal, Gaston Grimal, but I'd rather my name . . ."

"Of course. I only want to ask you if anything struck you about the behavior of your assailant. Give yourself a moment to reflect."

"I've been reflecting for half a hour. All my papers . . ."

"There is a good chance of recovering them. Your assailant?"

"He seemed to me like a young man of good family, not a hooligan."

"Were you far from a street lamp?"

"Not very far. The same as here to the next room. He looked as frightened as I was. So much so that I very nearly . . ."

"Resisted?"

"Yes. Then I thought that accidents easily happen and . . ."

"Anything else? What sort of suit was he wearing?"

"A dark suit, probably navy blue."

"Crumpled?"

"I don't know."

"Thank you, Monsieur Grimal. I'd be very surprised if between now and the morning a patrol doesn't find your wallet on the sidewalk. Without the money, of course."

It was a detail that Maigret hadn't thought of, and he reproached himself. Alain Lagrange had got hold of a revolver, but he could have had very little money in his pocket, to judge by the kind of life that was led on Rue Popincourt.

He left his office abruptly and went into the radio room, where there were only two men on duty.

"Put out a general call for me to police stations and cars."

Less than half an hour later all the stations in Paris were listening in.

"Report to Superintendent Maigret any armed holdup or attempted holdup taking place in the past twenty-four hours. Urgent."

He repeated it, gave the description of Alain Lagrange.

"Probably still in the Gare du Nord and Boulevard de la Chapelle area."

He did not return directly to his office, but went through to the hotels section.

"Just have a look and see if you haven't got the name Alain Lagrange somewhere. Probably in a second-class hotel."

It was worth trying. Alain hadn't given his name to Mme Maigret. There was a chance that he had slept somewhere the previous night. Since his identity wasn't known, why should he not have written his real name on the register?

"Will you wait, Superintendent?"

"No. Let me have the answer upstairs."

The specialists had returned from Rue Popincourt with their cameras, but the inspectors had remained over there. At half past midnight Maigret had a telephone call from the Police Commissioner.

"Nothing new?"

"Nothing definite, so far."

"What about the papers?"

"They'll publish only the bulletin. But once the first editions are out, I'm expecting a flood of reporters."

"What do you think, Maigret?"

"Nothing yet. The Delteil brother was determined it was a political crime. I politely dissuaded him."

The Chief Commissioner telephoned as well, and even Rateau, the Examining Magistrate. They all slept badly that night. As for Maigret, he had no intention of going to bed.

It was quarter past one when he received a more surprising call.

This one didn't come from the Gare du Nord area, or

72

even from the center of the city, but from the Neuilly police station.

Over there they had been speaking about Maigret's call to a policeman just returned from his beat, and the man, scratching his head, had finally mumbled:

"Perhaps I'd better call him."

He had told his story to the sergeant on duty. The sergeant had encouraged him to call the Superintendent. It was a young policeman, who had been in uniform only a few months.

"I don't know if it will interest you," he said, much too close to the instrument, so that his voice vibrated. "It was this morning, or, rather, yesterday morning, seeing it's past midnight. . . . I was on duty on Boulevard Richard-Wallace, on the edge of the Bois de Boulogne, almost opposite the Bagatelle. It's only from this evening that I'm on nights. . . . There was a row of buildings, all the same. It was about ten o'clock. . . . I had stopped to look at a big car of some foreign make, which had a license plate I didn't know. . . . A young man came out of a building behind me, the one with the number 7B. . . . I didn't pay any attention, since he was walking naturally, in the direction of the corner. . . . Then I saw the concierge coming out with an odd look on her face.

"As it happens, I know her a little. I talked with her one day when I was taking a summons to someone who lives in the building. . . . She recognized me. . . .

" 'You look worried,' I said to her. And she replied: 'I wonder what that fellow wanted in my building.' She was looking in the direction of the young man, who was just turning the corner.

" 'He just passed by the lodge without asking for anyone,' she went on. 'He went toward the elevator, hesitated, then went up the stairs. Since I'd never seen him before, I ran after him. "Who do you want?" He had already gone up several steps. He turned around, surprised, as if he was afraid, and stood there a good while without replying.

" 'All he could find to say to me was: "I must have come to the wrong building." ' "

The policeman went on: "The concierge declares he stared at her in such a funny way that she didn't dare press him. But when he left, she followed him. Intrigued, I went myself to the corner of Rue de Longchamp. There wasn't anybody there any longer. The young man must have taken to his heels. It's only just now that they've shown me the photograph. I'm not sure, but I'd swear it's him. I was probably wrong to call you. The sergeant told me . . ."

"You've done perfectly right."

And the young policeman, who had his wits about him, added:

"My name is Emile Lebraz."

Maigret called Lapointe.

"Tired?"

"No, Chief."

"Stay in my office and take any messages. I hope to be back here in three-quarters of an hour. If there's anything urgent, call me at Boulevard Richard-Wallace, in Neuilly. Number 7B. The concierge should have a telephone. In fact, it would save time if you'd call and warn her I want to talk to her for a moment. Then she'll have time to get up and put on a robe before I arrive."

The run through the deserted streets took little time, and when he rang he found the lodge lighted, the concierge not in a robe, but fully dressed to receive him. It was a handsome building, and the lodge was a sort of living room. In the next room, to which the door was open, he could see a child asleep.

"Monsieur Maigret?" stammered the good woman, quite overcome at receiving him in person.

"I am very sorry to have wakened you. I would just like you to look at these photographs and tell me if the young man you caught on the stairs yesterday morning looks like any of them."

He had taken the precaution of bringing a handful of photographs of young men of about the same age. The concierge took no longer than the businessman from Clermont.

"That's him!" she said, pointing to Alain Lagrange.

"You're quite sure about it?"

"There's no mistaking him."

"When you caught up with him, he didn't threaten you at all?"

"No! It's odd that you should ask me that, because I've thought about it. It's more an impression, if you see what I mean. I don't want to state as a fact what I'm not certain of. When he turned around he didn't move, but I had an odd feeling inside me. In point of fact, it seemed to me he was wondering whether to kill me. . . ."

"How many tenants have you in the building?"

"There are two apartments on each floor. That makes fourteen for the seven floors. But there are two empty at the moment. One family left for Brazil three weeks ago —they are actually Brazilians, from the embassy—and a gentleman on the fifth died twelve days ago."

"Can you let me have a list of your tenants?"

"That's easy. I've got one already made up."

Water was boiling on a gas range, and after handing a

piece of typed paper to the Superintendent the concierge set about making some coffee.

"I thought you'd like a cup. At this hour . . . My husband, whom I had the misfortune to lose last year, wasn't exactly in the police, but he was in the Republican Guard."

"I see two names on the ground floor, the Delvals and the Trélos."

She smiled.

"The Delvals, that's right. They are importers, with offices on Place des Victoires. But Monsieur Trélo is all alone. Don't you know him? He's the movie comedian."

"Anyway, it's not them the young man was after, because, after hesitating by the elevator, he headed for the stairs."

"On the next floor, to the left, Monsieur Desquiens, whom you see on the list, is away at the moment. He's on vacation with his children, who have a place in the Midi."

"What does he do?"

"Nothing. He's rich. He's a widower, very polite and quiet."

"On the right, Rosetti?"

"Italians. She's a very beautiful person. They have three maids, plus a nurse for the baby, who is just over a year old."

"Profession?"

"Monsieur Rosetti's in automobiles. It was actually his car the policeman was looking at when I came out behind the young man."

"On the next floor? I'm sorry to keep you up so late."

"Not at all. Two lumps of sugar? Milk?"

"No milk. Thanks. Mettetal. Who's that?"

"Rich people, too, but they can't keep their maids, because Madame Mettetal, who's in bad health, goes for everybody."

Maigret was writing notes in the margin of the list.

"On the same floor I see Beauman."

"Diamond brokers. They are traveling. It's the season. I forward their mail to them in Switzerland."

"Next floor, on the right, Jeanne Debul. Single woman?"

"A single woman, yes."

The concierge had said this in the tone women generally use to speak of another woman against whom they have a grudge.

"What type of person?"

"You can hardly call her a type. She left yesterday about noon for England. I was really rather surprised she hadn't mentioned it."

"To whom?"

"To her maid, a good girl, who tells me everything."

"Is the maid up there now?"

"Yes. She spent part of the evening here in the lodge. She wasn't in a hurry to go to bed, because she's nervous and terrified of sleeping by herself in the apartment."

"You say she was surprised?"

"The maid, yes. The night before, Madame Debul came home in the small hours, as often happens with her. You notice how they say Madame, but I'm convinced she's never been married."

"What age?"

"The real one, or the one she pretends to be?"

"Both."

"The real one I know, seeing as I had her papers in my hands when she got her lease."

"How long ago?"

"About two years. Before that she lived on Rue Notre-Dame-de-Lorette. The fact is she's forty-nine and pretends to be forty. In the morning she looks her age. In the evening, why, heavens . . ."

"Does she have a lover?"

"It's not exactly what you might think. Otherwise she wouldn't be kept on in the place. The management is very strict on that point. I don't quite know how to put it."

"Try."

"She's not the same class as the other residents. Even so, she's not a person who gives a bad impression, if you see what I mean. Not a kept woman, for example. She's got money. She gets letters from her bank, from her stockbroker. She could be a widow or a divorcée having a good time."

"Does she entertain?"

"Not gigolos, if that's what you have in mind. Her legal adviser comes from time to time. Women friends, as well. Sometimes couples. But she's more a woman who goes out than one who entertains at home. In the morning she stays in bed, till noon. In the afternoon she sometimes goes into town, always extremely well dressed, rather quietly even. Then she comes back to put on her evening dress, and I don't pull the cord to let her in till well after midnight. There's another odd thing besides, which her maid, Georgette, tells me. She spends a lot of money. Her furs alone are worth a fortune, and she always wears a diamond ring on her finger as big as that. Even so, Georgette says she's petty, and spends a large part of her time going over the household accounts."

"When did she leave?"

"About half past eleven. That's what surprised Georgette. At that time, her mistress ought still to have been in bed. She was asleep when she had a telephone call. Right afterward, she had a railway timetable brought to her."

"This was a short time after the young man tried to get into the house?"

"A little after, yes. She didn't wait for her breakfast and she packed herself."

"Large cases?"

"Only suitcases. No trunks. She's been around a lot."

"Why do you say that?"

"Because there were labels all over the cases, nothing but big hotels in Deauville, Nice, Naples, Rome, and other foreign places besides."

"She didn't say when she would be back?"

"Not to me. Georgette doesn't know anything about it either."

"She didn't ask her to have her mail forwarded?"

"No. She just called Gare du Nord to reserve a seat on the Calais express."

Maigret was struck by the persistence with which the words "Gare du Nord" had recurred since the beginning of the case. It was at the checkroom of Gare du Nord that François Lagrange had deposited the trunk containing the body of the Deputy. Again, it was in the neighborhood of Gare du Nord that his son had held up the businessman from Clermont-Ferrand.

This same Alain had slipped up the stairs of an apartment building on Boulevard Richard-Wallace, and, a little while later, a resident of the building had set off for Gare du Nord. Coincidence?

"You know, if you have the slightest desire to question Georgette, she would be absolutely delighted. She's so afraid of being alone that it would be a pleasure for her to have company."

And the concierge added:

"And especially company like yours!"

Before anything else Maigret wanted to finish with the residents of the building, and he pointed to their names patiently, one after the other. There was a film producer on the fourth floor, a genuine one this time, whose name was to be seen on walls all over Paris. Directly above him was a film director, well known, too, and, as though by chance, on the seventh floor there lived a scriptwriter, who did his daily dozen on the balcony every morning.

"Do you want me to go and warn Georgette?"

"I would like to make a telephone call first."

He called Gare du Nord.

"Maigret here, from the Police Judiciaire. Tell me, do you have a train for Calais around midnight?"

It had been about half past eleven when the businessman was held up on Rue de Maubeuge.

"At twelve-thirteen."

"Express?"

"It connects with the Dover Mail at half past five. It doesn't stop on the way."

"You don't remember issuing a ticket to a young man by himself?"

"The clerks who were in the ticket offices then have gone to bed."

"Thank you."

He called the Harbor Police in Calais, gave the description of Alain Lagrange.

"He's armed!" he added, just in case.

Then, without expecting too much, he announced, after emptying his cup of coffee:

"I'll go up and see Georgette. Warn her."

To which the concierge replied, with a malicious smile:

"You be careful. She's a pretty girl!"

She added:

"And she likes handsome men!"

5

ROSY-COMPLEXIONED, with ample breasts, she was in her pajamas, of candy-pink crepon, washed so often that they allowed dark shadows to show through. One would have said that her body, too rounded everywhere, was still not fully developed, and with her complexion, too fresh for Paris, she reminded one of a gosling which has not yet lost its down. When she opened the door to him, he caught the smell of her bed, of armpits.

He had let the concierge telephone her to wake her and say he was on his way up. She couldn't have got through right away, because, when he reached the third floor, the bell was still ringing in the apartment.

He waited. The telephone was too far from the landing for him to hear her voice. There were footsteps on the moquette, and she opened the door for him, not in the least embarrassed, without having taken the trouble to put on a robe. Perhaps she didn't have one? When she got up in the morning, it was in order to get to work, and when she undressed at night, it was to go to bed. She was blond, her hair all untidy, and there were still traces of lipstick on her lips.

"Sit down there."

They had crossed the hall, and she had switched on only a large standing lamp in the living room. She had chosen for herself a large sofa of delicate green, where she was half stretched out. The air coming in through the high French window billowed the curtains. She was watching Maigret with the solemnity of a child examining an important grownup whom people have told her a lot about.

"I didn't picture you quite like that," she finally admitted.

"How had you pictured me?"

"I don't know. You are better."

"The concierge told me you wouldn't mind if I came up and asked you a few questions."

"About Madame?"

"Yes."

That didn't surprise her. Nothing could have surprised her.

"How old are you?"

"Twenty-two years old, six of them in Paris. You can go ahead."

He began by showing her the photograph of Alain Lagrange.

"You know him?"

"I've never seen him."

"You're sure he's never come to see your mistress?"

"Not since I've been with her. Young people aren't her type, whatever you might think."

"Why should people think the opposite?"

"Because of her age."

"Have you been in service with her long?"

"Since she set up house here. That makes it nearly two years."

"You didn't work for her when she was living on Rue Notre-Dame-de-Lorette?"

"No. I applied the day she moved out."

"Did she still have her previous maid?"

"I didn't even meet her. She started fresh, you might say. The furniture, the bits and pieces, everything was new."

For her, this seemed to have one meaning, and Maigret thought he interpreted her innuendo correctly.

"You don't like her?"

"She's not the kind of woman one can like. Besides, it doesn't matter to her."

"What do you mean?"

"She thinks she's good enough. She doesn't take the trouble to be nice. When she talks to you, it's not for your benefit, but just because she wants to talk."

"You don't know who telephoned her just before she suddenly decided to leave for London?"

"No. She answered the telephone herself. She didn't mention any name."

"Did she seem surprised, annoyed?"

"If you knew her, you'd realize she never shows what she feels."

"You don't know anything about her past?"

"Except that she lived on Rue Notre-Dame-de-Lorette. She's friendly with me, and she goes through all the accounts with a fine-tooth comb."

From the way she spoke, that explained everything,

84

and this time, again, Maigret felt that he understood her meaning.

"In fact, in your opinion, she's not a lady?"

"Certainly not. I've worked with real ladies and I know the difference. I've also worked in the Place Saint-Georges area with a kept woman."

"Has Jeanne Debul been kept?"

"If she has been, she isn't any longer. She's certainly rich."

"Did men come to see her?"

"Her masseur came every other day. She was on friendly terms with him, too, and called him Ernest."

"Anything between them?"

"She's not interested."

Her pajama top was of the kind you slip over your head, very short, and as Georgette lay back on the cushions, her skin showed above her waistband.

"You don't mind if I smoke?"

"I'm sorry," he said, "but I haven't any cigarettes."

"There are some on the table. . . ."

She found it natural for him to get up and offer her a pack of Egyptian cigarettes belonging to Jeanne Debul. While he held the match, she puffed inexpertly at the cigarette, blowing out the smoke like a beginner.

She was pleased with herself, pleased at having been awakened by a man as important as Maigret, who was listening to her with attention.

"She's got plenty of men and women friends, but they seldom come here. She calls them up, mostly uses their Christian names. She sees them in the evening at cocktail parties, or in restaurants and nightclubs. I've often wondered if she didn't keep a house before. You see what I mean?"

"And the people who do come here?"

"Her legal adviser, chiefly. She sees him in her study. He's a lawyer, Gibon, who doesn't come from this neighborhood, but lives in the Ninth Arrondissement. So she knew him before, when she was in the same district. Then there's a slightly younger man who's with the bank, and she discusses her investments with him. He's the one she calls when she has instructions to give about her stocks."

"You never see a man named François Lagrange?"

"Carpet Slippers!"

She broke off with a laugh.

"It's not me who calls him that. It's the mistress. When I tell her he's here, she grumbles:

" 'That old Carpet Slippers again!'

"He always says, to announce himself:

" 'Ask Madame Debul if she can see Baron Lagrange.' "

"Does she see him?"

"Nearly always."

"Which means often?"

"Say, about once a week. There are some weeks when he doesn't come at all, others when he comes twice. Last week he came twice on the same day."

"About what time?"

"Always in the morning, about eleven o'clock. Apart from Ernest, the masseur, he's the only one she sees in her bedroom."

And, as he registered her point:

"It's not what you think. Even for the lawyer she dresses. I must say she dresses well, in a very quiet way. It's actually what struck me right away: what she's like in bed, in her room, and what she's like when she's

86

dressed. It's two different people. She doesn't speak in the same way: you might say that even her voice changes."

"Is she more common in bed?"

"Yes. Not only common. I can't think of the word."

"Is François Lagrange the only one she receives like that?"

"Yes. She shouts to him, no matter what state she's in:

" 'Come in, you!' As if they were old friends . . ."

". . . or accomplices?"

"If you like. Until I go out, they don't talk about anything important. He sits down timidly on the edge of an armchair, as though afraid of creasing the satin."

"Does he have papers, a briefcase, with him?"

"No. He's a proper gentleman. He's not my type, but I think he's so distinguished."

"You've never overheard their conversations?"

"It isn't possible with her. She guesses everything. She's got sharp ears. She's the one who does most of the listening at doors in this house. When I happen to be on the phone, I can be almost sure that she's somewhere around, spying on me. If I'm taking a letter to mail, she says to me:

" 'Who are you writing to now?'

"And I know she looks at the address. You know the type?"

"I see."

"There's something you haven't seen yet that may give you a surprise."

She jumped to her feet, threw the butt of her cigarette into the ashtray.

"Come with me. Now you've seen the living room. It's

furnished in the same style as all the other living rooms in the building. One of the best decorators in Paris took on the job. Here's the dining room, in modern style, too. Wait till I put on the light."

She pushed open a door, flicked a switch, stood out of the way to let him see a bedroom entirely in white satin.

"Now here's how she dresses in the evening."

In an adjoining room, she opened some closets and ran her hands over the silk of a neat array of dresses.

"So. Now come this way!"

She went in front of him down a hallway, and the crepon of her pajamas was caught between her buttocks. She opened another door, flicked another switch.

"There!"

It was a little office at the back of the apartment, which might have belonged to a businessman. Not the least feminine trace was to be seen. There was a metal file cabinet painted green, and behind the revolving chair there was an enormous safe of fairly recent design.

"It's here that she spends part of her afternoons and sees the lawyer and the man from the bank. Look . . ."

She was pointing to a pile of papers: *The Stock Exchange Courier*. True, Maigret noticed a racing paper beside them.

"Does she wear glasses?"

"Only in this room."

There was a pair of them, big round glasses with tortoise-shell frames, on a blotter with leather corners.

Mechanically he tried to open the file cabinet, but it was locked.

"Every night when she comes in, she goes and puts her jewels in the safe."

"What else does it contain? Have you ever seen inside?"

"Deeds mostly. Papers. Then there's a little red diary she often looks at."

From the desk Maigret picked up one of those indexes in which people jot down the telephone numbers they use often, and started going through its pages. He read out the names in an undertone. Georgette explained:

"The milkman . . . The butcher . . . The hardware store on Avenue de Neuilly . . . Madame's shoemaker . . ."

When, instead of a surname, there was only a Christian name, she would smile, satisfied.

"Olga . . . Nadine . . . Marcelle . . ."

"What did I tell you?"

Men's Christian names, too, but fewer of them. Then some names the maid did not know. Under the heading "banks," there were no fewer than five establishments entered, including an American bank on Place Vendôme.

He searched, without finding it, for the name Delteil. There were certainly an André and a Pierre somewhere. Did these refer to the Deputy and his brother?

"After seeing the rest of the apartment and the closet, were you expecting to find this?"

He said no, to please her.

"Aren't you thirsty?"

"The concierge was kind enough to make me some coffee."

"You won't have a little something?"

She led him back to the living room, turning out the lights behind her, and, as if the interview were likely to last a lot longer, took her place on the sofa again, since he had refused a drink.

"Does your mistress drink?"

"Like a man."

"Which means a lot?"

"I've never seen her drunk, except once or twice coming home in the small hours. But she pours herself a whisky right after her morning coffee, and has two or three more in the course of the afternoon. That's why I say she drinks like a man. She takes her whisky almost straight."

"She hasn't told you which hotel in London she will be staying at?"

"No."

"Or how long she expects to stay?"

"She told me nothing. She didn't take half an hour over her packing and dressing."

"How was she dressed when she left?"

"In her gray suit."

"Did she take any evening dresses with her?"

"Two."

"I don't think I've any more questions to ask you, and I'll let you go to bed."

"Already? Are you in a hurry?"

She deliberately uncovered a bit more of her body between the two parts of her pajamas, and deliberately, too, crossed her legs in a certain way.

"Do you often have to do your investigations at night?"

"Sometimes."

"You really don't want anything to drink?"

She sighed.

"Personally, now that I'm awake, I won't be able to go to sleep again. What time is it?"

"Getting on for three o'clock."

"At four it starts to get light, and the birds begin to sing."

He got up, sorry to disappoint her, and perhaps she still had hopes that he was not intending to leave, but only to come over to her. It wasn't until she saw him going toward the door that she got up in turn.

"You'll be coming back?"

"Possibly."

"You'll never bother me. Just give two little rings, then one long one. I'll know it's you and I'll open the door. When I'm alone I don't always open it."

"Thank you, mademoiselle."

Once again he caught the smell of bed, of armpits. One of the large breasts brushed against his sleeve with a certain insistence.

"Good luck!" she called to him softly, when he was on the stairs.

And she leaned over the banister to watch him go down.

At the Police Judiciaire he found Janvier waiting, having spent several hours at the rooms on Rue Popincourt. He looked worn out.

"How did it go, Chief? Did he talk?"

Maigret shook his head.

"I left Houard over there, just in case. We turned the apartment upside down, without getting much out of it. I've got only this to show you."

Maigret first poured himself a glass of brandy, then passed the bottle to the inspector.

"You'll see. It's rather odd."

In a rough paper cover, which had been torn from the back of a school exercise book, were some press clippings, some of them illustrated with photographs.

Frowning, Maigret read the headlines and ran through the stories, while Janvier watched him with a curious expression.

All the articles, without exception, were about the Superintendent, and some dated back seven years. They were reports of cases, published day by day, with, often, a summary of the court proceedings.

"Notice anything, Chief? While I was waiting for you, I took the trouble to read them from beginning to end."

Maigret noticed something he preferred not to mention.

"You could swear, couldn't you, that they've chosen the cases where you seemed to be more or less defending the guilty party."

One of the articles was headed: *"The Kind-hearted Superintendent."*

Another was devoted to testimony by Maigret to a high court, in the course of which all his replies showed his sympathy for the young man who was being tried.

Even clearer was another article, which had appeared the previous year in a weekly. It did not deal with any particular case, but with the question of guilt in general, and was titled: *"Maigret's Humanity."*

"What do you think of it? This file proves the fellow has been following you for a long time, has some interest in what you do or say, in your character."

Some words were underlined in blue pencil, among them the words "leniency" and "understanding."

And there was a passage entirely circled—one in which a reporter described the last morning of a man condemned to death, and revealed that after refusing a priest the condemned man asked for the favor of a final interview with Superintendent Maigret.

"You don't like it?"

He had in fact become more solemn, more intent, as though this discovery was opening up new horizons for him.

"You found nothing else?"

"Some bills. Unpaid, of course. The Baron owes money all over. The coal seller hasn't been paid for last winter. Here's a photo of the Baron's wife with his first child."

The print was a bad one. The dress dated it, and so did the hair style. The young woman posing for it had a melancholy smile. Perhaps it was the period when that was the fashion, in order to look distinguished. Yet Maigret felt certain that, simply through seeing this picture, anyone would have realized this woman was not destined for happiness.

"In a wardrobe, I found one of her dresses, pale-blue satin, and a boxful of baby clothes, too."

Janvier had three children, the youngest of them not a year old.

"My wife keeps only their first pair of shoes."

Maigret picked up the telephone.

"Police Infirmary!" he said in a low voice. "Hello! Who's speaking?"

It was the nurse, a redhead he knew.

"Maigret here. How's Lagrange? What did you say? I can't hear you clearly."

She was saying that her patient, who had been given an injection, had gone off to sleep almost immediately after the doctor's departure. Half an hour later she had heard a slight noise and had gone over on tiptoe to see what it was.

"He was crying."

"Didn't he speak to you?"

"He heard me, and I put on the light. The tears were still shining on his cheeks. He looked at me in silence for a while, and I had the feeling he was hesitating over whether to confide in me."

"Did he seem to you to be in his right senses?"

She, too, hesitated.

"It's not for me to judge," she countered, beating a retreat.

"Then what?"

"He made a move to take my hand."

"Did he take it?"

"No. He started whimpering, and kept on repeating, always the same words: 'You won't let them hit me, will you? . . . I don't want to be hit.' "

"That all?"

"Finally, he became excited. I thought he was going to jump out of bed, and he began to cry out: 'I don't want to die! . . . I don't want to! . . . I mustn't be left to die! . . .' "

Maigret hung up, turned to Janvier, opposite him, who was fighting against sleep.

"You can go home to bed."

"And you?"

"I've got to wait up till half past five. I want to know if the boy actually took the Calais train."

"Why should he have taken it?"

"To catch up with someone in England."

On Wednesday morning, Alain had stolen his gun from him, and had provided himself with ammunition. On Thursday he went to Boulevard Richard-Wallace, and half an hour later Jeanne Debul, who knew his fa-

94

ther, had a telephone call and set off in a hurry for Gare du Nord.

What was the young man doing during the afternoon? Why didn't he leave at once? Couldn't it be presumed to be only for lack of money?

To get some, by the only means at his disposal, he had to wait till nightfall.

It so happened he attacked the businessman from Clermont-Ferrand not far from Gare du Nord, a short time before the departure of the Calais train.

"By the way, I was forgetting to tell you there was a call about the wallet. It's been found in the street."

"Which street?"

"Rue de Dunkerque."

Still near the station.

"Without the money, of course."

"Before you leave, get the passport office on the phone. Ask them if they've ever issued a passport in the name of Alain Lagrange."

In the meantime he went and planted himself in front of the window. It was not yet day, but that gray, cold hour that comes before sunrise. In a sort of dull green mist the Seine flowed by, almost black, and a bargeman was washing down the deck of his boat, moored to the quay. A tug was going silently downstream, on its way to fetch its string of barges.

"He applied for a passport eleven months ago, Chief. He wanted to go to Austria."

"So his passport is still valid. You don't need a visa for England. You didn't find it among his things?"

"Nothing."

"No change of clothes?"

"He can only have one decent suit and he's got that on. There was another in his wardrobe, worn to threads. All the shoes we saw had holes in them."

"Go to sleep."

"You're sure you don't need me any longer?"

"Certain. Besides, there are still two men in the office."

Maigret wasn't conscious of dozing off in his arm-chair. When he suddenly opened his eyes, because the tug he had noticed a short while ago was returning upstream and whistling before negotiating the bridge with its seven barges behind it, the sky was pink and gleams of reflected light could be seen from various rooftops. He looked at his watch, picked up the telephone.

"Harbor Police, Calais!"

This took a little time. The Harbor Police did not reply at once. The inspector who eventually came to the phone was out of breath.

"Maigret, Police Judiciaire, here."

"I know what you're after."

"Well?"

"We've just finished examining the passports. The boat hasn't left the dock yet. My colleagues are still there."

Maigret heard the siren blasts from the mail boat, which was about to depart.

"Young Lagrange?"

"We haven't found anything. No one resembling him. There were very few passengers, and it was easy to check."

"Have you still got the list of the people who left yesterday?"

"I'll go and get it from the office next door. Will you hold on?"

When he spoke again, it was to say:

"I don't see any Lagrange on yesterday's departures either."

"It's not Lagrange I want. Look for a Madame Jeanne Debul."

"Debul . . . Debul . . . D . . . D . . . Here we are. . . . Daumas . . . Dazergues . . . Debul, Jeanne Louise Clementine, forty-nine, living at Neuilly-sur-Seine, 7B Boulevard . . ."

"I know. What destination address does she give?"

"Savoy Hotel, London."

"Thank you. You're sure that Lagrange . . ."

"You may rest assured, Superintendent."

Maigret was hot, perhaps because of not having slept. He was in a bad mood, and it was as if to get even that he seized hold of the bottle of brandy. Then all of a sudden he picked up the telephone again, grunted:

"Le Bourget."

"I beg your pardon?"

"I asked you to get me Le Bourget."

His tone was offensive; the operator made a wry face and acted quickly.

"Maigret here, from the Police Judiciaire."

"Inspector Mathieu."

"Is there a plane to London during the night?"

"There's one at ten o'clock in the evening, another at twelve-forty-five, and then the first of the morning took off a few seconds ago. I can still hear it gaining altitude."

"Will you get a passenger list?"

"Which flight?"

"Twelve-forty-five."

"One moment."

It was seldom that Maigret was so unfriendly.

"You there?"

"Yes."

"Look for Lagrange."

"Right . . . Lagrange, Alain François Marie."

"Thank you."

"That all?"

Maigret had already hung up. On account of that cursed Gare du Nord, which had hypnotized him, he hadn't thought of a plane, so that by now Alain Lagrange, with his loaded revolver, had already been in London for some time.

His hand hovered over the desk for a moment before grasping the telephone receiver.

"Savoy Hotel, London."

He got through almost at once.

"Savoy Hotel. Reception speaking . . ."

He was getting tired of repeating his patter, his name and office.

"Can you tell me if a Madame Jeanne Debul arrived at your hotel yesterday?"

This took less time than with the police. The reception clerk had the list of guests for each day within his reach.

"Yes, sir. Room 605. You wish to speak to her?"

He hesitated.

"No. See if you had an Alain Lagrange last night."

This took hardly any longer.

"No, sir."

"I presume you ask for the passports of travelers on their arrival?"

"Certainly. We follow the regulations."

"So Alain Lagrange couldn't be staying with you under another name?"

"Only if he had a false passport. They are checked every night by the police, remember."

"Thanks."

He still had one call to make, and this one he particularly disliked, all the more because he was going to be obliged to use the not very good English he had learned at school.

"Scotland Yard."

It would have been a miracle if Inspector Pyke, whom he had entertained in France, had been on duty at such an hour. He had to be content with a stranger, who was slow to understand who he was, and answered him in a nasal voice.

"A Madame Jeanne Debul, aged forty-nine, is staying at the Savoy, room 605. . . . I would like to have her discreetly watched for the next few hours. . . ."

The faraway voice had a mania for repeating Maigret's last words, but with the right accent, as though to correct him.

"It's possible a young man may try to pay her a visit or waylay her. I'll give you his description. . . ."

The description provided, he added:

"He's armed; a Smith & Wesson Special. That gives you an excuse to detain him. I'm having his photograph sent to you by wire in a few minutes."

But the Englishman seemed unable to grasp what he was talking about, and Maigret was obliged to spell things out, to repeat the same things three or four times.

"Now what exactly do you want us to do?"

Faced with so much obstinacy, Maigret was sorry he had taken the precaution of calling the Yard, and felt like replying: "Nothing at all!"

He was bathed in sweat.

"I'll be there as soon as possible," he ended by saying.

"You mean you're coming to Scotland Yard?"

"I'm coming to London, yes."

"What time?"

"I don't know. I haven't got the airline schedule in front of me. . . ."

"You're coming by air?"

He finally hung up, exasperated, calling down every sort of curse on this civil servant he didn't know, who was probably really a very good man. What would Lucas have replied to a Yard inspector calling him up at six o'clock in the morning to tell him a story of the same type in bad French?

"It's me again! Get me Le Bourget once more."

A plane was leaving at eight-fifteen. That gave him time to go around to Boulevard Richard-Lenoir to change and even to shave and swallow his breakfast. Mme Maigret was careful not to ask him questions.

"I don't know when I'll be back," he said grumpily, with the vague intention of making her angry with him, so he could blame his temper on someone else. "I'm off to London."

"Ah!"

"Get my little suitcase ready, with a change of clothes and my shaving things. There ought to be a few English pounds at the bottom of the drawer."

The telephone rang. He was in the middle of putting on his tie.

"Maigret? Rateau here."

The Examining Magistrate, bright and early, who had spent the night in bed, who was doubtless delighted at being awakened by brilliant sunshine, and who, as he ate his croissants, was asking for news.

"What did you say?"

"I said I haven't got time: I'm taking the plane to London in thirty-five minutes."

"To London?"

"That's right."

"But what have you found out that . . ."

"I'm sorry to hang up; the plane won't wait."

He was in such a state of mind that he added:

"I'll send you some postcards."

By then, of course, the receiver was back on its rest.

THERE WERE CLOUDS as they approached the French coast, and they flew above them. Through a large break, a little while later, Maigret had a chance of glimpsing the sea, which sparkled like fishes' scales, and fishing boats trailing their foamy wake behind them.

His neighbor leaned over in a friendly way to point out some chalky cliffs to him, explaining:

"Dover ... Douvres ..."

He thanked him with a smile, and soon there was nothing more than an almost transparent mist between the earth and the plane. Only now and then did they fly into a large, luminous cloud, from which they emerged almost immediately, to find beneath them once more pastures dotted with tiny cows.

Finally the landscape rocked, and it was Croydon. It was also Mr. Pyke. For Mr. Pyke was there, awaiting his

French colleague. Not on the airstrip itself, as he doubt-less would have had the right to be, not away from the crowd, but with it, wisely, behind the barrier separating passengers from relatives and friends waiting for them.

He made no gesticulation, didn't wave his handker-chief. When Maigret looked in his direction, he merely nodded his head, as he must do every morning on meet-ing his colleagues at the office.

It was years since they had seen each other, and twelve or thirteen years since the Superintendent had set foot in England.

He followed the line of people, suitcase in hand, into a building where he had to go through Immigration, then through Customs. Mr. Pyke was still there, behind a glass panel, in his dark-gray suit, which looked a little too tight for him, and his black felt hat, a carnation in his buttonhole.

He could have come in here as well, told the Immigra-tion official: "It's Superintendent Maigret, who's come to see us. . . ."

Maigret would have done that for him at Le Bourget. He did not mind, however, understanding that it was, on the contrary, a sort of tact on his part. Actually, he felt rather ashamed of his anger that morning with the policeman at the Yard. The fact that Mr. Pyke was there showed that the man had not done his job so badly, had even showed initiative. It was only half past ten. To reach Croydon in time, Pyke must have left London almost as soon as he arrived at his office.

Maigret was coming out of the room. The dry, hard hand was extended.

"How are you?"

Pyke went on, in French, which was a sacrifice on his

part, since he spoke it with difficulty and hated making mistakes:

"*J'espère que vous allez* . . . enjoy . . . How do you say it? . . . *Jouir* . . . *Oui, jouir de cette journée resplendissante.*"

It was in fact the first time Maigret had been in England in summer, and he wondered if he had ever seen London in real sunshine.

"I thought you would rather go by car than in the airline bus."

He did not speak to him about his investigation, made no reference to it, and that was again all part of his sort of tact. They took their seats in a Yard Bentley, driven by a man in uniform, and the latter, scrupulously respecting the speed limits, didn't jump any traffic lights.

"Pretty, isn't it?"

Pyke was pointing to some rows of small red-brick houses, which under gray skies would have looked gloomy, but which, in the sunshine, were trim, rather gay, each with a square patch of lawn slightly larger than a sheet between the front door and the fence. One could tell how he relished this prospect of suburban London, where he lived himself.

The red-brick houses were succeeded by yellow houses, then brown houses, then more red-brick ones. It was beginning to be very hot, and in some little gardens automatic hoses were playing.

"I was forgetting to let you have this."

He handed Maigret a piece of paper on which there were notes, written in French.

Alain Lagrange, age nineteen, office worker, checked in at 4:00 a.m. at Gilmore Hotel, opposite Victoria Station, without luggage.

Slept till eight o'clock, then went out.

First went to Astoria Hotel and made inquiries about Mme Jeanne Debul.

Then went to Continental Hotel, then to Claridge's, still asking the same question.

Appears to be following an alphabetical list of big hotels.

Has never been to London before. Does not speak English.

Now it was Maigret who merely nodded his thanks, and he was more annoyed with himself than ever for his unkind thoughts about the policeman that morning.

After a long silence and several rows of identical houses, Pyke began to speak:

"I took the liberty of reserving you a hotel room, because we have a lot of tourists at the moment."

He handed his colleague a slip bearing the name "Savoy" and the number of the room. Maigret very nearly paid no attention to it. Then the number struck him: 604.

So they had thought of putting him just opposite Jeanne Debul.

"Is that woman still there?" he asked.

"She was when we left Croydon. I had a report by telephone just as your plane was beginning to land."

Nothing else. He was satisfied, not so much with having proved to Maigret that the British police are efficient as with showing him England beneath an indisputable sun.

When they entered London and passed big red buses, when they saw women in light dresses on the sidewalks, he could not help murmuring:

"That's really something, isn't it?"

And, as they approached the Savoy:

"If you aren't busy, could I come and pick you up for lunch at about one? From now until then I will be in my office. You can call me."

That was all. He let him enter the hotel alone, while the uniformed chauffeur handed his suitcase to one of the porters.

Did the reception clerk recognize him after twelve years? Did he know him purely by his photographs? Or was it just flattery? Or the fact that his room had been reserved through Scotland Yard?

"Did you have a good journey, Monsieur Maigret?"

"Very good, thank you."

The immense lobby, where at every hour of the day and night there were people in deep armchairs, always overawed him a little. On the right, flowers were being sold. Every man had one in his buttonhole, and probably under the influence of Pyke's good humor, Maigret bought himself a red carnation.

He remembered that the bar was on the left. He was thirsty. He went toward the glass-paneled door, tried in vain to open it.

"At half past eleven, sir!"

His face clouded. It was always the same abroad. Details that enchanted him; then, all of a sudden, others that infuriated him. Why the devil hadn't he the right to have a drink before half past eleven? He hadn't been to bed all the night before. His head felt thick, and the sun was making him slightly giddy. Perhaps it was the motion of the plane as well?

As he was going toward the elevator, a man he didn't know came up to him.

"The lady has just had her breakfast taken up. Mr.

Pyke told me to keep you informed. Should I wait in case you want me?"

It was a man from the Yard. Maigret thought him elegant, not out of place in this luxurious hotel, and he, too, wore a flower in his buttonhole. His was white.

"The young man hasn't appeared?"

"Not so far, sir."

"Would you watch the lobby and warn me the moment he arrives?"

"It'll be some time before he gets to the letter S, sir. I think Inspector Pyke has posted one of my colleagues at the Lancaster Hotel."

The room was vast, with a pearl-gray adjoining sitting room. The windows gave onto the Thames, where just at that moment a boat was passing, the same kind as the river steamers of Paris, with two decks covered with tourists.

Maigret was so hot that he decided to take a shower and change. He all but called Paris for news of the Baron, changed his mind, dressed again, half opened the door. Room 605 was opposite. The sunlight could be seen under the door, which meant the curtains had been opened. Just as he was going to knock, he heard the noise of water in the bathroom, and he began to pace up and down the hall, smoking his pipe. A chambermaid passing by looked at him curiously. She must have mentioned him at the office, for a boy in uniform came and had a look at him, too. Then, seeing from his watch that it was eleven-twenty-four, he took the elevator and was at the door of the bar at the very second it was being opened. Other men as well, who must have been waiting for this moment in the armchairs in the lobby, were in an equal hurry.

"Scotch?"

"All right."

"Soda?"

His expression must have shown that he thought the drink didn't have much taste, for the barman suggested:

"A double, sir?"

Things were better already. He had never suspected it could be so hot in London. He went to get some fresh air for a few minutes in front of the big revolving doors, looked at the time again, and went over to the elevator.

When he knocked at the door of 605, a woman's voice inside called: "*Entrez!*"

Then, probably thinking it was the boy coming to take away her tray:

"Come in!"

He turned the handle, and the door opened.

He found himself in a room bright with sunshine, where a woman in a robe was seated before her dressing table. She didn't look at him right away. She went on brushing her brown hair, and she had hairpins between her teeth. It was in the mirror that she saw him. Her brows contracted.

"What do you want?"

"Superintendent Maigret, of the Police Judiciaire."

"Does that give you the right to walk into other people's rooms?"

"You told me to come in."

It was hard to tell her age. She must have been very beautiful once, and something of it remained. In the evening, with the lights low, she would probably give that impression, especially if her mouth didn't take on the hard twist it had at the moment.

"You can start by taking your pipe out of your mouth."

He did so, awkwardly. He hadn't thought about his pipe.

"Then, if you have something to say, get it over with quickly. I don't see what business the French police can have with me. Especially here."

She was still not facing him, and it was disquieting. She must have known it, and lingered at her dressing table, watching him in the mirror. Standing up he felt too big, too massive. The bed was not made. There was a tray with the remains of breakfast, and he could see only a small armchair, in which he could scarcely accommodate his large thighs.

He announced, looking at her himself by means of the mirror:

"Alain is in London."

Either she was very strong-minded or else the name meant nothing to her, since she did not falter.

He went on in the same tone:

"He's armed."

"Did you cross the Channel just to tell me that? I presume you've come from Paris? What name did you say? I mean yours."

He was convinced she was playacting, in the hopes of annoying him.

"Superintendent Maigret."

"Which district?"

"Police Judiciaire."

"You're looking for a young man whose name is Alain? He's not here. Search the room if that would reassure you."

"It's he who's looking for you."

"Why?"

"That's just what I'd like to ask you."

This time she got up, and he saw that she was almost as tall as he was. She was wearing a robe of heavy salmon-colored silk, which showed a still-attractive figure. She went to get a cigarette from a side table, lighted it, rang for service. For a moment he thought it was with the intention of having him thrown out, but when the waiter appeared she simply said:

"Scotch. Without ice. With water."

Then, when the door had closed, she turned toward the Superintendent.

"I've nothing to say to you. I'm sorry."

"Alain is the son of Baron Lagrange."

"Possibly."

"Lagrange is one of your friends."

She shook her head, as though she felt sorry for him.

"Listen, Superintendent, I don't know what you've come here to do, but you're wasting your time. Probably there is some mistake about the person concerned."

"You really are Jeanne Debul?"

"That's my name. You want to see my passport?"

He made a sign that there was no need.

"Baron Lagrange has been in the habit of paying visits to your apartment on Boulevard Richard-Wallace, and before that probably on Rue Notre-Dame-de-Lorette."

"I see that you are well informed. Tell me now, how does the fact that I've known Lagrange explain your pursuing me to London?"

"André Delteil is dead."

"You mean the Deputy?"

"Was he one of your friends as well?"

"I don't think I ever met him. I've heard people talk about him, like everyone else, because of his questions in the Chamber. If I have seen him, it was in some restaurant or nightclub."

"He's been murdered."

"Judging by his political methods, he must have made himself a certain number of enemies."

"The murder was committed in François Lagrange's apartment."

There was a knock at the door. It was the waiter with the Scotch. She drank one straight off, like a person used to taking alcohol every day at the same time, and, glass in hand, went over and sat on the chair, crossed her legs, pulled the sash of her robe.

"That's all?" she asked.

"Alain Lagrange, the son, got hold of a gun and some ammunition. He went around to your house yesterday, a short while before you left so abruptly."

"Say that word again."

"Ab-rupt-ly."

"Because you know, I suppose, that, the evening before, I had no intention of coming to London?"

"You hadn't told anyone."

"Do you tell your plans to your maid? Presumably it was Georgette you questioned?"

"It's unimportant. Alain went to your house."

"No one told me about it. I didn't hear the bell ring."

"Because on the stairs he was caught by the concierge and did an about-face."

"He told the concierge it was me he wanted to see?"

"He said nothing."

"Can you be serious, Superintendent? Was it really just to tell me these fancy tales that you made the trip?"

"You had a telephone call from the Baron."

"Really!"

"He brought you up to date about what had happened. Or perhaps you already knew?"

He was hot. She wasn't giving him any opening, still as calm, as fresh as ever in her appearance for the morning. From time to time she would sip from her glass, without thinking of offering him anything to drink, and she left him standing, feeling awkward.

"Lagrange is under arrest."

"That's his affair and yours, isn't it? What does he have to say about it?"

"He tries to pretend he's mad."

"He always has been a little mad."

"He's nonetheless a friend of yours?"

"No, Superintendent. You can save your ingenuity. You won't make me talk, for the excellent reason that I have nothing to say. If you care to examine my passport, you will see that I do sometimes spend a few days in London. Always at this hotel, where they will confirm it. As for Lagrange, poor man, I've known him for some years."

"Under what circumstances did you meet him?"

"That's none of your business. Under the most banal circumstances. I will say, however, that it happened as a man and a woman meet one another."

"He was your lover?"

"You are a man of the utmost delicacy."

"Was he?"

"Suppose he was, for an evening or a week, or even a month. . . . It was twelve or fifteen years ago. . . ."

"You remained good friends?"

"Ought we to have quarreled or fought?"

"You used to receive him in the mornings, in your bedroom, when you were still in bed."

"It's morning now, my bed's unmade, and you're in my room."

"You did business with him?"

She smiled.

"What business, for Heaven's sake? Don't you know that all the business old Carpet Slippers talked about existed only in his imagination? Didn't you take the trouble to find out about him? Go to Le Fouquet, to Maxim's, to any bar on the Champs-Elysées, and they'll tell you. It wasn't worth taking the boat or the plane just for that."

"Did you give him money?"

"Is that a crime?"

"A lot?"

"You will observe that I am patient. I could have had you thrown out a quarter of an hour ago, because you've no right to be here or to question me. I want, however, to repeat, once and for all, that you are on the wrong track. I knew Baron Lagrange once, when he was still handsome and fooled everyone. I met him again later on the Champs-Elysées, and he treated me as he does everybody."

"Which means?"

"He sponged. Ask anyone about him. He's the sort of man who's always short of a few hundred francs in order to bring off the most stupendous deal and make himself rich in a few days. Which means he hasn't enough to pay for the apéritif he's drinking at the moment or for the métro to get home. I behaved like the others."

"And he badgered you at your home?"

"That's all."

"Nevertheless, his son is looking for you."

"I've never seen him."

"He's been in London since last night."

"In this hotel?"

This was the only occasion when her voice was a little less firm, betraying a certain anxiety.

"No."

He hesitated. He had to choose between two solutions, and he leaned toward the one he thought would be better.

"The Gilmore Hotel, opposite Victoria Station."

"How can you be sure it's me he's looking for?"

"Because all this morning he has been turning up at a whole string of hotels and asking for you. He seems to be going in alphabetical order. In less than an hour he will be here."

"Then we'll find out what he wants from me, won't we?"

There was a slight quaver in her voice.

"He is armed."

She shrugged her shoulders lightly, got up, looked at the door.

"I suppose I should thank you for having the kindness to watch over me."

"There's still time."

"For what?"

"For talking."

"We've been doing nothing but that for the last half hour. Now I must ask you to leave me alone so that I can dress."

She added, in a voice that did not ring altogether true, with a little laugh:

"If this young man is really coming to pay me a visit, I'd better be ready!"

Maigret left without saying anything more, his shoulders rounded, annoyed with himself and with her, because he had got nothing out of her and he had a feeling that, throughout the interview, Jeanne Debul had kept the upper hand. With the door closed again, he paused in the hallway. He would have liked to know if she was telephoning or showing signs of sudden activity.

Unfortunately, a chambermaid, the same one who had seen him prowling about the hallway earlier, came out of a nearby room and stared at him. Feeling disconcerted, he began to walk toward the elevator.

In the lobby he rejoined the Yard man installed in one of the armchairs, his eyes riveted on the revolving doors. He sat down next to him.

"Any sign?"

"Not yet."

At that hour there were many arrivals and departures. Cars drew up incessantly in front of the hotel, bringing not only travelers but also Londoners coming to lunch or simply to have a drink at the bar. They were all very happy. They all had the same look of delight as Pyke at such an exceptional day. Groups began to form. There were three or four people around the reception desk constantly. Women, in armchairs, were waiting for their escorts, whom they then followed into the dining room.

Maigret remembered another way out of the hotel, giving onto the Embankment. If he were in Paris . . . It would all be so easy! Pyke had put himself at his disposal in vain; he did not want to abuse his offer. The fact was, here, he was always afraid of making himself look ridiculous. Did Inspector Pyke have the same humiliating sensation during his stay in France?

Upstairs in the hallway, for example . . . in France the

presence of a maid would not have perturbed him. He would have told her some story, probably that he was from the police, and would have continued his vigil.

"Lovely day, sir!"

Even that was beginning to jar on him. These people were too pleased with their exceptional sun. Nothing else counted any more. The passers-by in the street were walking as though in a dream.

"D'you think he'll come, sir?"

"It's likely, isn't it? The Savoy is on the list."

"I'm a bit afraid Fenton may have been clumsy."

"Who's Fenton?"

"My colleague . . . the one Inspector Pyke sent to the Lancaster. He was to sit down like me opposite the reception desk and wait. Then, when the young man left, to follow him."

"He's no good?"

"He's not bad, sir. He's a very good man. Only, he is red-haired and he has a mustache. So that once he's been seen, he's easily recognized."

The man looked at his watch, sighed.

Maigret himself was watching the elevators. Jeanne Debul came out of one of them, wearing a pretty two-piece spring dress. She appeared to be completely at ease. On her lips she had the slight smile of a woman who knows she is pretty and well dressed. Several men followed her with their eyes. Maigret had noticed the big diamond she was wearing on her finger.

In the most natural way in the world, she took a few steps into the lobby, looking at the faces around her, then put her key on the reception desk, and hesitated.

She had seen Maigret. Was she acting for his benefit? There were two places you could lunch: the big dining room on one side, which adjoined the lobby and had bay windows that looked out on the Thames, and the grill, less vast, less solemn, where there were more people and where the windows allowed you to see the hotel entrance. It was the grill she made for finally. She said a few words to the maître d'hôtel, who showed her promptly to a little table near a window.

At the same moment the Yard man next to Maigret was saying:

"That's him. . . ."

The Superintendent looked quickly into the street through the revolving doors, saw no one resembling the photograph of Alain Lagrange, opened his mouth to ask a question.

Before he even framed it, he understood. A small man with very red hair and a flamboyant mustache was nearing the door.

It was not Alain who was referred to, but Fenton. In the lobby he looked around for his colleague, went up to him, and, ignoring the presence of Maigret, asked:

"He hasn't come?"

"No."

"He came to the Lancaster. So I followed him. He went into the Montreal. I wonder if he noticed me. He had turned around once or twice. Then, all of a sudden, he jumped into a taxi. I lost a minute finding one for myself. I tried at five other hotels. He hadn't . . ."

One of the pageboys was leaning toward Maigret.

"The head of reception would like a word with you," he murmured in a low voice.

The head of reception, in a morning coat and with a flower in his buttonhole, was holding a telephone receiver in his hand.

He winked at Maigret, a sign the Superintendent thought he understood. Then he said into the instrument:

"I'll give you the man on duty."

Maigret took the receiver.

"Allo!"

"*Vous parlez français?*"

"*Oui* . . . Yes . . . I speak French. . . ."

"I'd like to know if Madame Jeanne Debul is staying at your hotel."

"Who is calling?"

"One of her friends."

"You wish to speak to her? I can have you put through to her room."

"No . . . No . . ."

The voice seemed far away.

"Her key is not here. So she must be in. I imagine she will be down before long."

"Thank you."

"Can I . . ."

Alain had already hung up. He wasn't such a fool, after all. He must have realized that he was being followed. Rather than show himself in person at various hotels, he had adopted the device of telephoning from a booth or a bar.

The head of reception was holding another receiver in his hand.

"Another for you, Monsieur Maigret."

This time it was Pyke, asking him to have lunch with him.

"I'd better stay here."

"Have my men been successful?"

"Not entirely. It's not their fault."

"Have you lost track of him?"

"He's definitely coming here."

"Anyway, they are at your disposal."

"I'll keep the one who's not called Fenton, if you don't mind."

"Keep Bryan. Excellent. He's intelligent. Perhaps this evening?"

"Perhaps this evening."

He rejoined the two men, who were still chatting. They fell silent on his arrival. Bryan must have told Fenton who he was, and the red-haired fellow was looking contrite.

"Thank you, Mr. Fenton. I've picked up the tracks of the young man. I won't need you any more today. Will you have a drink?"

"Never on duty."

"You, Mr. Bryan, I would like you to go and lunch in the grill, near that woman wearing a two-piece dress with small blue flowers. If she leaves, try to follow her."

A faint smile stole over Bryan's lips as he watched his companion depart.

"Count on me."

"You can charge the bill to my account."

Maigret was thirsty. He had been thirsty for more than half an hour. Because the too-deep armchairs were making him hot, he rose, wandered around the lobby, ill at ease in the midst of people speaking English who all had a reason to be there.

How many times did he see the doors revolve, each time sending a reflection of sunlight across one of the walls? Yet again. There was a constant coming and going. Cars were stopping, driving off, old London taxis, comfortable and picturesque, Rolls-Royces and Bentleys with impeccable chauffeurs, small models like racing cars.

Thirst was parching his throat, and from where he was he could see the bar, full of people drinking, and the pale Martinis, which, from afar, looked so fresh in their ice-cold glasses, the whiskies the customers standing at the bar were holding in their hands.

If he went over there, he would lose sight of the door. He approached it, went away again, regretted having dismissed Fenton, who could at least have taken over the watch for a few minutes.

As for Bryan, he was busy eating and drinking. Maigret was beginning to feel hungry as well.

He sat down again, sighing, as an old gentleman with white hair, in the chair next to his, pressed an electric bell, which Maigret hadn't noticed. A few moments later a waiter in a white jacket was bending toward him.

"A double Scotch with ice!"

There! It was as simple as that. It had never occurred to him that he could be served in the lobby.

"The same for me. I suppose you haven't any beer?"

"Yes, sir. What sort of beer would you like?"

The bar had every kind of beer, Dutch, Danish, German, and even a French export beer Maigret had never heard of.

In France he would have ordered two glasses at once, he was so dry. Here he didn't dare. And it infuriated him not to dare. It was humiliating to be thus intimidated.

Were the waiters, the maîtres d'hôtel, the pageboys, the porters more imposing than those in a big Paris hotel? It seemed to him that everyone was watching him, that the old gentleman, his neighbor, was studying him with a critical eye.

Was Alain Lagrange going to make up his mind one way or the other, to come or not?

It wasn't the first time this had happened to him: Maigret all of a sudden, without any plausible reason, was losing confidence in himself. What was he doing here, in actual fact? He had passed the night without sleeping. He had been to drink coffee in a concierge's lodge, then he had listened to the tales of a big girl in rose-colored pajamas who showed him a patch of her stomach and tried hard to make herself interesting.

What else? Alain Lagrange had lifted his revolver, threatened a passer-by in the street and stolen the passer-by's wallet before taking the plane to London. At the Police Infirmary the Baron was acting like a madman.

What if he really was mad?

Suppose Alain did appear at the hotel? What was Maigret going to do? Accost him politely? Tell him he wanted an explanation?

What if he tried to escape, if he showed fight? What sort of a figure would he cut, in front of all these Englishmen smiling at their sunshine, attacking a young boy? Perhaps it would be him they would grab hold of?

It had happened to him once in Paris—when he was a young man, though, and still on the beat. Just as he was reaching out for the shoulder of a thief in the line of people coming out of the métro, the fellow started shouting: "Help!" And it was Maigret the crowd had held until the police arrived.

He was still thirsty, hesitated to ring, then finally pressed the white button, convinced that his white-haired neighbor thought him an ill-bred fellow who drank glasses of beer one after the other.

"A . . ."

He thought he recognized a profile outside, said, without thinking:

"A whisky-and-soda."

"Certainly, sir."

It wasn't Alain. From close up, he didn't look like him at all, and, besides, he joined a girl waiting for him at the bar.

Maigret was still there, thoroughly torpid, with an unpleasant taste in his mouth, when Jeanne Debul came out of the grill in fine form, and reached the revolving doors.

Outside she waited for one of the doormen to whistle for a taxi. Bryan was following, looking sprightly himself, and he winked at Maigret as he passed.

He seemed to be saying: "Don't worry!" He got into a second taxi.

If Alain Lagrange had been considerate, he would have arrived now. Jeanne Debul was no longer there. So there was no danger of his charging at her and firing his revolver. The lobby was quieter than it had been for the past half hour. People had eaten. Looking more pink-faced, they went off one after the other about their business, or to walk down Piccadilly or Regent Street.

"Same again, sir?"

"No. This time I would like a sandwich."

"I'm sorry, sir. We are not allowed to serve anything to eat in the lobby."

He could have wept with rage.

"Well, give me anything you like. Same again, then!"

Too bad, on top of everything else. It wasn't his fault.

7

AT THREE O'CLOCK, at half past three, at four Maigret
was still there, as uncomfortable as when, after days and
days of stormy heat, people look irritably at one another,
so cross that one expects to see them open their mouths
to breathe like fish out of water.

The difference was that he was the only one in this
state. There was not the slightest sign of a storm in the
air. The sky above the Strand remained a pretty, airy
blue, without any trace of violet, with occasionally a
little white cloud that floated in space like a feather es-
caped from an eiderdown.

At odd moments he caught himself examining his
neighbors as though to vow to them his personal hatred.
At others an inferiority complex weighed on his stomach
and gave him a shifty look.

They were all too smart, too sure of themselves. The
most exasperating of all was the head of reception, with

his smooth morning coat, his collar which no drop of sweat would ever soften. He had shown friendliness toward Maigret, or perhaps it was pity, and from time to time he gave him a smile at once conspiratorial and encouraging.

He seemed to be saying, above the coming and going of the anonymous travelers: "We are both victims of professional duty. Can't I do anything for you?"

Maigret would probably have replied: "Bring me a sandwich."

He was sleepy. He was hot. He was hungry. When, a few minutes after three, he had rung for another glass of beer, the waiter looked as shocked as if he had taken off his coat in church.

"I'm sorry, sir. The bar is closed until half past five, sir!"

The Superintendent muttered something like:

"Savages!"

And ten minutes later, ill at ease, he had gone up to a pageboy, the youngest and least imposing one.

"Could you go and buy me a bar of chocolate?"

He was unable to last any longer without eating, and so it was that he consumed, in little bits, a bar of milk chocolate concealed in the depths of his pocket. Mustn't he look, in the lobby of this palatial hotel, like one of those caricatures of a French detective, whom the Parisian journalists call "hobnail socks"? He caught himself looking in the mirrors, found himself ugly, ill-dressed. Pyke, well, he didn't look like a policeman, but like a bank manager. Or, rather, an assistant manager. Or a trusted clerk, a meticulous clerk.

Would Pyke wait, as Maigret was doing, without even knowing that anything was going to happen?

At twenty of four the head of reception made a sign to him.

"Paris on the line for you. I suppose you would prefer to take the call here?"

Some telephone booths stood in a row in a room to the right of the lobby, but from there he wouldn't be able to watch the entrance.

"That you, Chief?"

It was good to hear old Lucas's voice.

"What's the latest?"

"The revolver's been found. I thought I'd better tell you."

"Go ahead."

"Just before noon I went and paid a call at the old man's place."

"Rue Popincourt?"

"Yes. I started poking around in the corners on the off chance. I couldn't find anything. Then I heard a baby crying in the courtyard, so I leaned out of the window. The rooms, you remember, are on the top floor, with a rather low ceiling. A gutter collects the water from the roof, and I noticed that you could reach this gutter with your hand."

"The gun was in the gutter?"

"Yes. Just below the window. A small revolver, Belgian make, a very nice job, initialed A. D."

"André Delteil."

"Exactly. I made inquiries. The Deputy had a license to carry weapons. The numbers coincide."

"It's the weapon that was used?"

"The expert has just sent in his report by telephone. I was waiting for it before calling you. The answer is yes."

"Any fingerprints?"

"The dead man's and François Lagrange's."

"Has anything else happened?"

"The evening papers have long stories. The corridors are swarming with reporters. I think one of them, who got wind of your going to London, has taken a plane. Examining Magistrate Rateau has called two or three times to find out if you'd sent any news."

"That all?"

"It's wonderful weather."

Him, too!

"Have you lunched?"

"Very well, Chief."

"I haven't! Hello! Don't cut us off, miss. Are you listening, Lucas? I want you, just in case, to keep an eye on the building at Number 7B on Boulevard Richard-Wallace. Also question the taxi drivers to find out if any of them drove Alain Lagrange . . . Listen! It's the son; you've got his picture."

"I understand."

"Find out, as I was saying, if one of them took him on Thursday morning to Gare du Nord."

"I thought he didn't leave till during the night, by air."

"Doesn't matter. Tell the Chief I'll call him as soon as I have some news."

"You haven't found the boy?"

He thought it best not to reply. He didn't much like to admit that he had had Alain on the telephone, that for hours his movements had been followed, minute by minute, through the streets of London, but that they were no further ahead.

Alain Lagrange, with the large revolver stolen from Maigret in his pocket, was somewhere around, probably not far away, and all the Superintendent could do was wait, and watch the crowd coming and going around him.

"I'll hang up."

His eyelids were prickling. He didn't dare sit down in an armchair, for fear of dropping off to sleep. The chocolate turned his stomach.

He went for a breath of air outside the main entrance.

"Taxi, sir?"

He no longer had the right to take a taxi, or the right to go for a walk, the right to do anything, except stay there and act the fool.

"Lovely weather, sir!"

Scarcely had he gone back into the lobby when his archenemy, the head of reception, called him again, a smile on his lips, a telephone in his hand.

"For you, Monsieur Maigret."

It was Pyke.

"I've just received some news from Bryan by telephone and am passing it on to you."

"Thanks very much."

"The lady had herself dropped at Piccadilly Circus and went up Regent Street to look at the shop windows. She didn't appear to be in a hurry. She went into two or three shops to buy a few things, which she had sent to the Savoy. Would you like the list?"

"What sort of things?"

"Lingerie, gloves, shoes. Then she went through to Old Bond Street to come back down Piccadilly, and half an hour ago went into a movie theater with a continuous showing. She's there now. Bryan is still watching her."

Another detail, which would not have struck him at any other time, but which put him in a bad temper: instead of phoning him, Maigret, Bryan had called his own chief in the hierarchy.

"Are we having dinner together?"

"I'm not sure. I'm beginning to doubt it."

"Fenton is very upset about what happened."

"It was no fault of his."

"If you need one of my men, or several of them . . ."

"Thanks."

What on earth was that Alain creature doing? Was Maigret to believe he had been mistaken from beginning to end?

"Can you get me the Gilmore Hotel?" he asked, when Pyke hung up.

By the expression on the head of reception's face, he gathered that it was not a first-class hotel. This time he had to speak English, because the man on the other end of the line did not understand a word of French.

"Has Monsieur Alain Lagrange, who came to your hotel very early this morning, been in during the day?"

"Who's speaking?"

"Superintendent Maigret, of the Police Judiciaire in Paris."

"One moment, please."

Someone else was called, with a more impressive voice, who was obviously more important.

"Can I help you? This is the manager of the Gilmore speaking."

Maigret repeated his patter.

"May I ask you why you are making the inquiry?"

He launched into an involved explanation, for want of the right English words. The head of reception finally took the receiver from his hands.

"Can I help?"

It took him only a couple of sentences, in which the words "Scotland Yard" were mentioned. When he hung up, he was delighted.

"These people always distrust foreigners a bit. The manager of the Gilmore was just wondering if he ought to warn the police. The young man took his key and went up to his room about one o'clock. He didn't stay there very long. Later, a chambermaid, who was cleaning a room on the same floor, reported that her skeleton key, which she had left in the door, had disappeared. Does that tell you anything?"

"Yes."

The episode actually somewhat altered the picture he had formed of young Alain. The boy's wits had been at work all that morning. He had figured that if a maid's skeleton key opens all the doors of one hotel, there is a good chance that it will open the doors of another hotel as well.

Maigret went and sat down. When he looked at the time, it was five o'clock. He went back suddenly to the reception desk.

"Do you think a skeleton key of the Gilmore Hotel would open the doors here?"

"It's unlikely."

"Would you mind checking that none of your maids has lost her skeleton key?"

"I imagine they would have informed the floor manager, who would herself have . . . One moment . . ."

He saw to a gentleman who wanted to change his suite because there was too much sun in his, then disappeared into an office nearby, where several telephone bells could be heard ringing.

When he came back, he was no longer quite so patronizing, and his brow was furrowed.

"You're right. A bunch of keys has disappeared from the sixth floor."

"In the same way as at the Gilmore?"

"In the same way. While they're doing the rooms, the staff have a mania, despite regulations, for leaving the keys in the door."

"How long ago did this happen?"

"Half an hour. Do you think this means trouble for us?"

And the man looked at the lobby with the same anxious expression as a captain who is responsible for his ship. Must he not, at all costs, avoid the smallest incident that would dull the splendor of so fine a day?

In France, Maigret would have said to him: "Give me another skeleton key. I'm going upstairs. If Jeanne Debul comes back, keep her here for a moment and warn me."

Not so here. He was sure they wouldn't let him enter a suite taken by someone else without a warrant.

He was prudent enough to wander around the lobby for a while. Then he decided to wait for the bar to open, since it was only a matter of minutes, and, not watching the revolving doors, he propped himself up there long enough to drink a couple of glasses of beer.

"You're thirsty, sir."

"Yes."

That "yes" was glum enough to squash the smiling barman.

He maneuvered to leave the lobby without being seen from the reception desk, took the elevator, worried by the thought that his whole plan from now on depended on the mood of a male or female staff member.

The long hallway was empty when he started down it, and he slowed up and stopped completely until he saw a door open and a valet in a striped vest appear, a pair of dancing shoes in his hand.

Then, with the self-assurance of a resident without any ulterior motive, whistling between his teeth, he headed toward number 605, fumbled in his pockets, looked disconcerted.

"Valet, please."

"Yes, sir?"

He was still fumbling. It wasn't the same valet as in the morning. The relief shift must have taken over.

"Would you mind opening my door for me, to save me going down for my key?"

The other suspected nothing.

"With pleasure, sir."

Having opened the door, he did not look inside, where he would have seen a woman's robe hanging.

Maigret closed the door again, carefully, mopped his brow, walked into the middle of the room, where he said in his normal voice, as if he were making conversation:

"Well, now!"

He didn't go into the bathroom, of which the door was ajar, or look in the closets. He was disturbed, underneath, far more than he let it appear or his voice let it be suspected.

"Here we are, my boy. Now we're going to have a little chat together."

He sat down heavily in the chair, crossed his legs, drew a pipe from his pocket and lighted it. He was convinced Alain Lagrange was hiding somewhere, perhaps in one of the closets, perhaps under the bed.

He also knew that the young man was armed, that he was highly strung, that his nerves must be at breaking point.

"All I ask you is not to do anything silly."

It was from the direction of the bed that he thought he

heard a slight sound. He wasn't quite sure of it, didn't lean forward.

"Once upon a time," he went on, as if he were telling a story, "I was an eyewitness to an extraordinary scene, near my home, on Boulevard Richard-Lenoir. It was in summer, too, one evening when it had been very hot, when it was still hot and the whole neighborhood was out of doors."

He was speaking slowly, and anyone coming in at that moment would have taken him at the very least for an eccentric.

"I don't know who saw the cat first. I seem to remember it was a little girl, who ought to have been in bed at that hour. Night was beginning to fall. She pointed to a dark shape in a tree. As always, passers-by stopped. From my window, where I was leaning out, I could see them gesticulating. Others joined the group. Soon there were a hundred people at the foot of the tree, and I finally went to see for myself as well."

He broke off to remark:

"Here, we are alone: that makes it easier. What was drawing the bystanders on the boulevard was a cat, a big tabby cat, crouched right at the end of a branch. It seemed frightened at finding itself there. It can't have realized that it had climbed so high. It didn't dare make a move to turn around. It didn't dare jump either. The women, with their noses in the air, felt sorry for it. The men were trying to devise a way of getting it out of its unfortunate predicament.

" 'I'll go and fetch a double ladder!' said a workman who lived opposite.

"They put up the ladder. He climbed it. It was three feet too short for him to reach the branch. But even so, at the sight of his outstretched arm the cat hissed with rage and tried to claw him.

"A boy suggested: 'I'll climb up.'

" 'You can't. The branch isn't strong enough.'

" 'I'll shake it, and all you'll have to do is hold out a sheet.'

"He must have seen firemen in the movies.

"It had become a real occasion. A concierge brought a sheet. The boy shook the branch, and the poor brute at the end of it hung on with all its claws and cast panic-stricken glances around.

"Everyone felt sorry for it.

" 'If we had a longer ladder . . .'

" 'Watch out! Perhaps it's angry. There's blood around its mouth.'

"It was true. They were sorry and they were afraid as well, you understand? No one wanted to go to bed without seeing the end of this business with the cat. How to get it into its head that it could let itself fall into the outstretched sheet without danger? Or that all it had to do was turn around?"

Maigret was almost expecting a voice to ask:

"What happened?"

But there wasn't any question, and he went on by himself:

"They got it in the end; a tall, thin fellow crept along the branch and, with the aid of a stick, managed to make the cat fall into the sheet. When they opened it, the animal jumped out so quickly that you could scarcely see it cross the street and disappear into a ventilator. That's all. . . ."

This time he was sure there had been a movement under the bed.

"The cat was afraid because it didn't know that no one wished it any harm."

Silence. Maigret drew on his pipe.

"I don't wish you any harm either. It isn't you who killed André Delteil. As for my gun, it's not a very serious matter. Who knows? At your age, in the state you were in, I would perhaps have done the same. It's my fault, after all. Oh, yes. If, that day, I hadn't gone and had an apéritif before lunch, I would have got home half an hour earlier, when you were still there."

He was talking in a negative, almost sleepy tone of voice.

"What would have happened? You would have told me right out what you meant to tell me. After all, it was to speak to me that you came to my home. You couldn't know a revolver was lying on the mantelpiece. You wanted to tell me the truth and ask me to save your father."

He was silent rather longer this time, to give his words time to sink into the young man's head.

"Don't move yet. It isn't necessary. We are quite all right as we are. I only advise you to be careful with the gun. It's a special model, which the American police are very proud of. The trigger is so sensitive that you hardly have to touch it to set it off. I've never used it. It's a souvenir, you see."

He sighed.

"Now, I wonder what you would have said to me if I had come in to lunch a little earlier. You would have had to tell me about the body. . . . Wait . . . We're in no hurry. . . . First of all, I imagine you weren't in on Tuesday evening when Delteil paid your father a visit. If you had been there, things would have turned out differently. You must have come in when it was all over. Probably the body was hidden in the bedroom you use as a storeroom, perhaps already in the trunk. Your father said nothing to you. I bet you don't talk much to each other, you two?"

He caught himself waiting for a reply.

"Well! Perhaps you suspected something, perhaps not. Be that as it may, in the morning you discovered the body. You kept quiet. It's difficult to broach a subject like that with one's father.

"Yours was all in, sick.

"Then you thought of me, because you read the newspaper clippings your father collected.

"So, here's more or less what you'd have said to me:

" *'There's a body in our apartment. I don't know what happened, but I know my father. To begin with, there's never been any weapon in our apartment.'*

"For I bet there never has been one. Isn't that so? I don't know your father very well, but I'm sure he's very scared of revolvers.

"You would have gone on:

" *'He's a man who couldn't harm anyone. That won't stop him from being the one they're going to accuse. He won't tell the truth, because a woman is involved.'*

"If it had happened like that, I would have helped you, of course. We would have found out the truth together.

"By this time it's almost certain that the woman would be in prison."

Was he hoping it would happen there and then? He mopped his brow, watching for a reaction that did not come.

"I had a longish talk with your sister. I don't think

you like her very much. She's an egoist, who thinks only of herself. I haven't had time to see your brother, Philippe, but he must be even harder than she is. Both of them have a grudge against your father for the childhood they had, whereas your father actually did all he could. It's not given to everyone to be strong. You, you understood. . . ."

Under his breath, he was saying to himself: "Don't let her come back just yet, Lord!"

For then it would probably be like the cat on Boulevard Richard-Lenoir, with the whole population of the Savoy around an adolescent at the end of his tether.

"You see, there are some things that you know and I don't know, but there are others that I know and you don't. Your father at this moment is in the Police Infirmary. That means he is under arrest, but people are wondering if he is in his right mind. When all's said and done, as usual, the psychiatrists disagree. They never do agree. What must be worrying him most is not knowing what's happened to you, or what you are going to do. He knows you, realizes you are capable of going through with your plans.

"As for Jeanne Debul, she's at the movies.

"It wouldn't help anyone for her to be killed coming back into her room. To start off with, it would be rather a bore, because it would be impossible to question her, and also because you would fall into the hands of the law of England, which in all probability would end up hanging you.

"There you are, young man.

"It's horribly hot in this room, and I'm going to open the window. I'm not armed; it's a mistake to imagine that all police inspectors and superintendents are armed.

Actually, they have no more right to be than other citizens.

"I'm not looking under the bed. I know you are there. I know almost everything you are thinking. It's difficult, of course! It's less spectacular than shooting at a woman and playing executioner!"

He went over to the window, which he opened, then leaned on the sill, his ears pricked, looking out. Nothing moved behind him.

"You haven't made up your mind?"

He became impatient, facing into the room again.

"You'll make me believe you are less intelligent than I thought! Where will it get you staying there? Speak up, idiot! After all, you are nothing but a young idiot. You haven't understood the first thing about this affair, and if you go on like this, it's you who'll end up by getting your father condemned. Leave my gun alone, do you hear? I forbid you to touch it. Put it on the floor. Now come out of there."

He seemed really angry. Perhaps in fact he was. In any case, he was in a hurry to get this unpleasant scene over.

As with the cat, so now, a false move would be enough, an idea passing through the young man's head.

"Hurry up. She's not going to be much longer coming back. It wouldn't be very smart to let her find us like this, you under the bed, me trying to make you come out. I will count up to three. . . . One . . . two . . . If at three you are not standing up, I shall telephone to the hotel detectives and . . ."

Then, at last, two feet appeared, worn-down soles, then cotton socks, the lower half of a pair of trousers Alain had ruffled up in crawling.

To make it easier for him Maigret turned back to the window, from where he heard a slithering on the floor, then the light noise of someone standing up. He didn't forget the young man was armed, but he was waiting to give him time to recover himself.

"Is it all over?"

He turned all the way around. Alain was standing before him, with dust on his blue suit, his tie askew, his hair in disorder. He was very pale, his lips were trembling, his eyes seemed to want to wander over the room.

"Give me back my gun."

Maigret held out his hand, and the young man fumbled in his right-hand pocket, held out his hand in turn.

"Don't you think it's better this way?"

There was a faint:

"Yes."

Then, right away:

"What are you going to do?"

"First of all, eat and drink. Aren't you hungry?"

"Yes. I don't know."

"Well, I'm very hungry, and there's an excellent grill-room on the ground floor."

He made for the door.

"Where have you put the skeleton key?"

He pulled out not one, but a whole bunch, from his other pocket.

"It would be better for me to hand them in to reception, since they might make a scene about it."

In the hallway he stopped in front of his own door.

"We'd better tidy ourselves up a little."

He didn't want a crisis. He knew that it was only hanging by a thread. That was why he was keeping the other's mind busy with small material details.

"Have you a comb?"

"No."

"You can use mine. It's quite clean."

That almost won him a smile.

"Why are you doing all this?"

"All what?"

"You know what I mean."

"Perhaps because I was a young man once myself. And had a father. Brush yourself off. Take off your coat. The bedspring hasn't been cleaned for a long time."

He himself washed his hands and face in cold water.

"I wonder if I shouldn't change my shirt again. I've sweated quite a bit today!"

He did, so that Alain saw him bare-chested, with his suspenders hanging over his thighs.

"Of course you haven't any luggage?"

"I don't think I can go into the grill as I am."

He examined him with a critical eye.

"Your clothes are certainly not very clean. Did you sleep in your shirt?"

"Yes."

"I can't lend you one of mine. It would be too big."

This time Alain smiled more openly.

"It's just too bad if the maître d' doesn't like it. We'll talk in a corner and try to get them to give us a little white wine, nice and cold. Perhaps they've got that."

"I don't drink."

"Never?"

"I tried once, and I was so sick I didn't start again."

"Have you got a girlfriend?"

"No."

"Why?"

"I don't know."

"Are you shy?"

"I don't know."

"Have you ever wanted to have a girlfriend?"

"Maybe. I think so. But I'm not very interested."

Maigret did not insist. He had understood. And, as they went out of the room, he put his big hand on his companion's shoulder.

"You gave me a fright."

"What about?"

"Would you have fired?"

"At whom?"

"At her."

"Yes."

"And yourself?"

"Perhaps. Afterward, I think I'd have done it."

They passed the valet, who turned around to look at them. Perhaps he had seen them coming out of number 604, whereas Maigret had gone into number 605?

The elevator deposited them on the ground floor. Maigret had his key in his hand as well as the bunch of passkeys. He went over to the reception desk. He was hoping for a little triumph over his archenemy in the too-well-cut morning clothes. How would it strike him seeing them together and receiving the skeleton keys?

Alas! It wasn't he who was standing behind the desk, but a tall, pale, fair-haired young man, who wore an identical morning coat and flower. He didn't know Maigret.

"I found this bunch of keys in the hallway."

"Thanks very much," he said, unconcernedly.

When Maigret turned around, Bryan was standing in the middle of the lobby. From the look in his eyes he seemed to be asking the Superintendent if he could have a word with him.

"Will you excuse me?" he asked Alain.

He went over to the English detective.

"You've found him? It's really him?"

"Yes."

"The lady has just come in."

"Has she gone up to her room?"

"No. She's in the bar."

"Alone?"

"She's chatting with the barman. What shall I do?"

"Can you bear to keep an eye on her for another hour or two?"

"Easily."

"If she looks like she's going out, warn me right away. I'll be in the grillroom."

Alain hadn't tried to run away. He was waiting, a little awkwardly, a little embarrassed, at the edge of the crowd.

"Enjoy your meal, sir."

"Thanks."

He rejoined the young man, whom he led toward the grill, saying:

"I'm ravenous."

And he caught himself adding, as he passed through a ray of sunshine slanting through a wide bay window:

"What wonderful weather!"

8

"YOU LIKE LOBSTER?"

Only Maigret's eyes appeared above the immense menu the maître d'hôtel had put in his hand, and Alain didn't know what to do with his, which, out of tact, he didn't look at.

"Yes, sir," he answered, as if at school.

"Well then, we'll treat ourselves to a lobster à l'Américaine. Before that I would like a plate of hors d'oeuvres. Waiter!"

His order given, he said:

"When I was your age, I preferred canned lobster meat, and when I was told this was heretical, I would reply that it had more taste. We had lobster once every six months, on special occasions, since we weren't rich."

He leaned back a little.

"You've suffered from not being rich, haven't you?"

"I don't know, sir. I would have liked my father not to have had to worry so much about bringing us up."

"You really don't want anything to drink?"

"Only water."

Nevertheless, Maigret ordered himself a bottle of wine, a Rhine wine, and glasses the color of absinthe, with long stems of a darker hue, were set before them.

The grillroom was lighted, but the sunlight lingered on outside. The room was filling rapidly, with maîtres d'hôtel and waiters in tails moving about noiselessly.

What fascinated Alain were the wheeled tables. They had brought one, laden with hors d'oeuvres, up to their table, and there were others, including some with pastries and desserts. Best of all was the enormous dome-shaped silver one, which opened like a box.

"Before the war, it used to hold a roast quarter of beef," explained Maigret. "I think it's here that I've eaten the best roast beef. Anyway, the most memorable. Now they've put a turkey in it. Do you like turkey?"

"I think so."

"If you've any appetite left after the lobster, we can have turkey."

"I'm not hungry."

They must have looked, the two of them together at their little table, like a rich uncle from the country giving a gala dinner to his nephew at the end of the school year.

"I lost my mother very young, too, and it was my father who brought me up."

"Did he take you to school?"

"He couldn't. He had to work. It was in the country."

"When I was very small, my father used to take me to school and come to fetch me home. He was the only man waiting at the door among the women. When he got back home, it was he who made supper for us all."

"There must have been times when you had servants."

"Did he tell you that? Have you talked to him?"

"I've talked with him."

"Is he worried about me?"

"I will call Paris soon so they can reassure him."

Alain didn't realize that he was eating with a good appetite, and he drank a large gulp of the wine, which the wine steward had served as a matter of course. He didn't make a face.

"That never lasted long."

"What?"

"Servants. My father so much wanted to change it all that he acted as if his wishes had come true from time to time. 'From now on, children,' he would announce, 'we're going to live like everyone else. Tomorrow, we move.' "

"Did you move?"

"Sometimes. We would go into a new apartment, where there was still no furniture. They would bring it when we were already there. We saw new faces, women my father had hired from an employment agency, and we called them by their first names. Then almost at once the shopkeepers would begin to troop in, and sheriffs, who would wait for hours thinking my father was out when he was only hiding in one of the rooms. Finally they would cut off the gas and the electric light. It's not his fault. He's very intelligent. He has heaps of ideas. Listen."

Maigret bent his head to hear better, his face relaxed, his eyes full of sympathy.

"There were years of that. . . . I remember that for a long time, perhaps two years, he went around to all kinds of offices with a scheme for enlarging and modernizing a Moroccan port. All he got was promises.

If that had come off, we would have gone to live over there and we'd have been very rich. When the plan reached the higher authorities, they shrugged their shoulders. They all but treated my father as if he were mad for wanting to establish a big port at that point. Now the Americans have done it."

"I understand."

Maigret knew that type of man so well! But could he show him up to his son for what he was? What was the point? The other two, the elder son and the daughter, had long ago seen the truth and had left, without feeling any gratitude for the big, weak, soft man who, after all, had brought them up. He couldn't look to those two for pity.

There was only Alain left to believe in him. It was odd, because Alain looked so much like his sister that it was disturbing.

"A few more mushrooms?"

"No, thank you."

Looking out was not without its fascination for him. It was the hour at which, as at lunch, cars followed one another without respite, waiting their turn to stop for a moment beneath the awning, where a doorman in mouse-gray livery would hurry to the car door. The difference from noon was that the people who got out of the cars were nearly all in evening dress. There were plenty of young couples, and whole families, too. Most of the women wore orchids.

The men were in dinner jackets, some in tails, and through the windows they could be seen coming and going in the lobby before taking their places in the main dining room, from which filtered the strains of the orchestra.

It was, to the very end, a marvelous day, with still enough light from the setting sun to lend an unreal hue to people's faces.

"Until what age did you go to school?"

"Fifteen and a half."

"High school?"

"Yes. I finished my third year and then left."

"Why?"

"I wanted to earn some money to help my father."

"Were you a good student?"

"Fairly. Except math."

"Did you find a job?"

"I worked in an office."

"Did your sister give your father the money she earned?"

"No. She used to pay for her board and lodging. She had it worked out exactly, without counting the rent, or the heating or the light. It was she who used up the most electricity, reading in bed part of the night."

"You handed over everything to him?"

"Yes."

"You don't smoke?"

"No."

The arrival of the lobster interrupted them for a while. Alain seemed relaxed now. From time to time, however, because he was sitting with his back to the door, he would turn around in that direction.

"What are you looking at?"

"To see if she's coming."

"You think she will come?"

"I saw you talking to someone and glancing toward the bar. I gathered from that that she was there."

"You know her?"

"I've never spoken to her."

"And does she know you?"

"She'll recognize me."

"Where has she seen you?"

"Two weeks ago on Boulevard Richard-Wallace."

"You went up to her apartment?"

"No. I was opposite, on the other side of the railings."

"Had you been following your father?"

"Yes."

"Why?"

Maigret had gone too fast. Alain was withdrawing.

"I don't see why you are doing all this."

"All what?"

With a glance, he indicated the grill, the table, the lobster, the luxuries that the man who ought logically to have clapped him in jail was lavishing on him.

"We had to eat, didn't we? I haven't had anything since this morning. What about you?"

"A sandwich, in a milk bar."

"So we're having dinner. Afterward we'll see."

"What'll you do?"

"We'll very likely take the plane to Paris. Do you like flying?"

"Not much."

"Have you been abroad before?"

"Not before. Last year I was to have spent two weeks in Austria at a vacation camp. An organization works an exchange program for young people of the two countries. I put my name down. They told me to get a passport. Then, when my turn came, I had sinus trouble and was in bed."

A silence.

He had returned to the thought that was uppermost

147

in their minds, and it only remained for him to bring it up again himself.

"Have you spoken to that person?"

"To whom?"

"To her."

"This morning, in her bedroom."

"What did she say?"

"Nothing."

"It's she who ruined my father, but you'll see, nothing can be done to her."

"You don't think so?"

"You wouldn't dare arrest her, would you?"

"Why?"

"I don't know. It's always like that. She's taken precautions."

"You know all about her dealings with your father?"

"Not exactly. It was only a few weeks ago that I learned what she is."

"Yet he's known her for a long time."

"He's known her since just after my mother died. At that time he didn't hide her from us. I don't remember anything about it myself, because I was only a baby, but Philippe told me. Father had told him he was going to marry again, which would be better for everybody, because there would be a woman to look after us. It didn't happen. Now that I've seen her, and know the sort of woman she is, I'm sure she was making a fool of him."

"Very possibly."

"Philippe says Father was miserable about it, that he often cried in bed at night. He went years without seeing her. Perhaps she left Paris. Or changed her address without telling him.

"Then about two years ago I noticed a change in my father."

"In what way?"

"It's difficult to say exactly. His whole attitude was no longer the same. He was gloomier and, above all, worried. When anyone came up the stairs he would tremble, and seem relieved when it was a shopkeeper, even one coming to dun him.

"My brother wasn't with us any longer by then. My sister had announced she would be leaving on the day she was twenty-one. It didn't all happen at once, you see. It was only now and again that I noticed the difference.

"In the old days, even in bars where I used to go and meet him to do errands for him, he used to drink only bottles of Vichy water. He started having apéritifs, and some evenings he came back very drunk, saying he had a headache.

"He didn't look at me in the same way any more, seemed embarrassed by my presence, and spoke impatiently to me."

"Eat up."

"I'm sorry; I'm not hungry any more."

"Dessert?"

"All right."

"It was then that you began to follow him?"

He hesitated before replying, and looked closely at Maigret, frowning, and at that moment he looked so like his sister that Maigret turned his eyes away.

"It was quite natural for you to try to find out what was happening."

"Even so, I don't know anything."

"Right. You know only that he often went to see this woman, especially in the late afternoon. You followed him to Boulevard Richard-Wallace, you admitted just now. You were down below, behind the railings of the Bois de Boulogne. Your father and the woman must have gone to a window in the apartment. Did she notice you?"

"Yes. She pointed at me with her finger. Probably because I was looking in the direction of the window."

"Your father told her who you were. Did he speak to you about it afterward?"

"No. I was expecting him to speak, but he didn't."

"And you?"

"I didn't dare."

"You found the money?"

"How do you know?"

"Isn't it true that in the evening you sometimes searched your father's wallet, not to take money, but to find out?"

"Not his wallet. He used to put it under his shirts, in the drawer."

"A lot?"

"Sometimes a hundred thousand francs, sometimes more, sometimes only fifty thousand."

"Often?"

"It varied. Once or twice a week."

"And the day after these evenings he would go around to Boulevard Richard-Wallace?"

"Yes."

"Then the money wasn't there any more?"

"She left him a few small notes."

Alain saw a gleam in Maigret's eye as he watched the door, but he had enough strength of mind not to turn around. He was not unaware that it was Jeanne Debul coming in.

Behind her, Bryan made a questioning gesture to the Superintendent, who in turn gave him to understand that he could stop trailing her.

If it was so late, it was because, on leaving the bar, she had gone up to change. Though she was not in an evening dress, she was wearing a fairly formal one, which must have come from a first-class dressmaker. On her wrist she had a wide diamond bracelet, and more diamonds at her ears.

She hadn't seen the Superintendent or Alain, and was following the headwaiter, while most of the women looked her up and down.

She was placed less than twenty feet away from them, at a little table almost facing them, and she sat down, glanced around as they handed her the menu, met Maigret's eye, and at once looked hard at his companion.

Maigret was smiling the smile of a man who has dined well, his mind at rest. Alain, blushing scarlet, didn't dare turn in her direction.

"Has she seen me?"

"Yes."

"What's she doing?"

"She's just defying me."

"What do you mean?"

"She's pretending to be at her ease, lighting a cigarette and leaning over to examine the hors d'oeuvres on a table beside her. Now she's talking with the headwaiter and making her diamonds sparkle."

"You won't arrest her!" he said with bitterness and a touch of defiance.

"I won't arrest her today, because, you see, if I were foolish enough to do so, she would get out of it."

"She'll always get out of it, while my father . . ."

"No. Not always. Here in England I am at a disadvantage, because I would have to prove that she has committed one of the crimes covered by the extradition laws. She won't stay in London forever. She needs Paris. She'll go back, and I will have had time to see about her. Even if it isn't right away, her turn will come. Sometimes we leave people at large for months, even years, under the impression that they are fooling us. You can look at her. You don't have to be ashamed. She's just showing off. Still, she'd rather be in your shoes than her own.

"Suppose I had left you under the bed. She would have gone up. By now . . ."

"Don't."

"You would have fired?"

"Yes."

"Why?"

Alain muttered between his teeth:

"Because!"

"Are you sorry?"

"I don't know. There's no justice!"

"Oh, yes, there's a sort of justice, and it does what it can. Obviously, if I were God the Father this evening, instead of being at the head of a special squad and having to account to my superiors, to the magistrate, to the prosecutor, even to the press, I would arrange this differently."

"How?"

"First of all, I would forget you stole my revolver. That I can still do. Then I would arrange for a certain businessman, from I can't remember where, to forget that he didn't lose his wallet but was forced to hand it over with a gun under his nose."

"It wasn't loaded."

"Are you sure?"

152

"I'd taken good care to remove the cartridges. I needed the money for getting to London."

"You knew the Debul woman was here?"

"I followed her that morning. First of all I tried going up to her apartment. The concierge . . ."

"I know."

"When I came out of the building there was a policeman at the entrance, and I guessed it was for me. I went around the block. When I got back, the policeman wasn't there any longer. I hid in the park, waiting for her to come out."

"To shoot her?"

"Perhaps. She must have telephoned for a taxi. I couldn't get near her. I was lucky enough to find another taxi coming from Puteaux. I followed her as far as the station. I saw her get on the Calais train. I didn't have enough money left to pay for a ticket."

"Why didn't you kill her when she was standing at the train compartment door?"

Alain shuddered, looked at him to see if he was being serious, mumbled:

"I didn't dare."

"If you didn't dare shoot when you were in a crowd, you probably wouldn't have shot her in her bedroom either. You had been following your father for several weeks, hadn't you?"

"Yes."

"Have you a list of people he went to see?"

"I could make one up from memory. He went several times to a little bank on Rue Chauchat, and also to a newspaper office, where he saw the assistant editor. He made a lot of telephone calls and kept turning around all the time to make sure he wasn't being followed."

"Did you realize what was going on?"

"Not right away. I happened to read a novel about it."

"About what?"

"You know perfectly well."

"Blackmail?"

"It was her."

"Of course. And that's why it'll take some time to get her. I don't know what kind of life she led before she moved to Boulevard Richard-Wallace. She probably got around and knew all kinds of people. A woman is better than a man at finding out little secrets, especially shameful secrets. When she was no longer young enough to carry on her sort of life, she got the idea of making money out of her bits and pieces of information."

"She made use of my father."

"Precisely. She wasn't the one who went and sought out the victims to demand money from them. It was a man about town who had no definite profession. People weren't overly surprised. They almost expected it."

"Why do you say that?"

"Because you must face the facts. Perhaps your father was still in love? I think he was. He's the sort of man to remain faithful to an infatuation like that. Jeanne Debul more or less provided his keep. He lived in fear of being caught. He was ashamed of himself. He didn't dare look you in the face any more."

Alain turned a hard face, with eyes full of hate, in the direction of the woman, who wore a thin, contemptuous smile.

"One strawberry tart."

"Aren't you having any?" protested Alain.

"I seldom eat dessert. Coffee and a *fine* for me."

He pushed his chair back a little, pulled his pipe from

his pocket. He was busy filling it when the headwaiter leaned toward him and said a few words in a low voice, waving an apology with his hands.

Then Maigret stuffed his pipe back into his pocket and stopped a passing cart that had cigars.

"Aren't you going to smoke your pipe?"

"Not allowed here! By the way, have you paid for your hotel room?"

"No."

"Have you still got the passkey you took from the hallway? Hand it to me."

He passed it to Maigret under the table.

"Is the tart good?"

"Yes . . ."

His mouth was full of it. He was just a child now, unable to resist sweet things, and at that moment he was entirely engrossed in his tart.

"Did he often see Delteil?"

"I saw him go around to his office twice."

Was it necessary to discover the whole truth? It was more than likely that the Deputy, whose wife was petitioning for a divorce and who was going to find himself without a penny, obliged to leave his big house on Avenue Henri-Martin, was trading on his influence. It was more serious for him than anyone else, because he had built up his political career by denouncing scandals and intrigues.

Had Jeanne Debul gone too far? Maigret had another idea on the subject.

"Your father didn't talk any longer about finishing with your kind of life?"

Despite the strawberry tart Alain lifted his head in sudden distrust.

"What do you mean?"

"In the old days, he used to announce periodically that everything was going to change. Then there was a time when he seemed to lose faith in his stars."

"Even so, he still hoped."

"Less strongly, though?"

"Yes."

"And recently?"

"He spoke three or four times about going to live in the Midi."

Maigret didn't go on. This was his affair. There was no point in explaining to the son what he deduced from it. Hadn't François Lagrange, who had been carrying out commissions for the Debul woman for two years and only picking up the crumbs, got it into his head to work on his own account?

Supposing Jeanne Debul ordered him to extract a hundred thousand francs from Delteil, who was a big shot . . . And the Baron had demanded a million? Or more? He was a man who liked talking in big figures, who had spent his life juggling with imaginary fortunes. . . .

Delteil decided not to pay.

"Where were you, on Tuesday night?"

"I went to the movies."

"Did your father encourage you to go out?"

He paused to think. This idea had come to him for the first time.

"I think he did. . . . He said to me . . . I seem to remember he spoke to me about a film being shown exclusively at the Champs-Elysées and . . ."

"When you came back, he'd gone to bed?"

"Yes. I went to say good night, as I always do; he

wasn't well. He promised me he would see the doctor."

"That struck you as quite normal?"

"No."

"Why?"

"I don't know. I was worried. I couldn't get to sleep. There was a strange smell in the house, a smell of American cigarettes. In the morning I woke up when it was hardly daybreak. I went around the apartment. My father was asleep. I noticed that the storeroom, which was my bedroom when I was small, was locked and the key wasn't in the door. I opened it."

"How?"

"With a hook. It's a trick I learned from my friends at school. You twist a thick bit of wire in a special way and . . ."

"I know. I've done it, too."

"I always kept one of those hooks in my drawer. I saw the trunk in the middle of the room and I lifted the lid."

It was best to move quickly now.

"Did you speak to your father?"

"I couldn't."

"You left at once?"

"Yes. I walked around the streets. I wanted to call on that woman."

There was one scene whose details would never be known unless the Baron gave up playing the madman, and that was the one enacted in the apartment between François Lagrange and André Delteil. It didn't concern Alain. There was no point in shattering the picture he had formed of his father.

The chances were very small that the Deputy had come with the intention of killing him. More than likely

157

he intended, if necessary by means of threats, to recover the documents that were being used to blackmail him.

Weren't the sides rather unevenly matched? Delteil was full of vigor. He was a man used to fighting, and all he had to oppose him was a big trembling hulk.

The documents were not in the apartment. Even if he had wanted to, Lagrange would have been unable to return them.

What had he done? He had probably wept, begged, asked to be forgiven. He had promised . . .

All the time, he was being hypnotized by the revolver that was threatening him.

It was he, by virtue of his very weakness, who had ended up winning the fight. How had he got hold of the weapon? By what ruse had he distracted the Deputy's attention?

However it came about, the fact remained that he no longer trembled. His turn now to speak loudly, to threaten.

Probably he hadn't pulled the trigger on purpose. He was too much of a coward, too used, ever since his schooldays, to walking about with his head hanging and receiving kicks in the behind.

"Finally I went to your apartment."

Alain turned toward Jeanne Debul, who was trying in vain to catch some of their conversation. The sounds that filled the grillroom, the noise of dishes, knives, forks, the hum of conversation, the laughter, and the music coming from the big room prevented her hearing.

"Shall we be going . . . ?"

There was a protest in Alain's eyes:

"Are you going to leave her there?"

The woman, too, was surprised to see Maigret pass by

without saying a word to her. It seemed too easy for her. Perhaps she had hoped for a scene, which would have given her plenty of scope.

In the lobby, where he finally took his pipe from his pocket and triumphantly stubbed out his cigar in the sand of a monumental ashtray, Maigret murmured:

"Will you wait here a second?"

He went up to the reception desk.

"What time is there a plane for Paris?"

"There is one in ten minutes, but you obviously can't catch that. The next is half past six in the morning. Shall I reserve a seat?"

"Two."

"What names?"

He gave them. Alain hadn't moved and was looking at the lights of the Strand.

"Just a moment. A telephone call to make."

He no longer had to do it from the reception desk; he could go into one of the booths.

"That you, Pyke? I'm sorry I couldn't lunch or have dinner with you. I won't see you tomorrow either. I'm going back during the night."

"On the half past six plane? I'll drive you there."

"But . . ."

"See you then."

It was better to let him do it; otherwise he would never be happy. Strange as it was, Maigret was no longer sleepy.

"Shall we have a stroll outside?"

"If you want to."

"Otherwise I won't even have set foot on a London sidewalk during my entire visit."

It was true. Was it because he was conscious of being

abroad? The streetlights seemed to him to have a different sort of light from the ones in Paris, another color, and even the air had a different smell.

The two of them walked along unhurriedly, looking at the movie entrances, the bars. After Charing Cross there was an enormous square with a column in the middle.

"Did you come this way this morning?"

"I think so. I seem to recognize it."

"Trafalgar Square."

It was pleasant, before leaving, to come across sights he recognized, and he took Alain as far as Piccadilly Circus.

"It only remains for us to go to bed."

Alain could have run away. Maigret wouldn't have lifted a finger to stop him. But he knew the young man wouldn't do so.

"Still, I would like a glass of beer. Do you mind?"

It wasn't so much the beer as the atmosphere of a pub that Maigret was looking for. Alain didn't drink anything, but waited in silence.

"You like London?"

"I don't know."

"Perhaps you'll be able to come back in a few months. It shouldn't really take as much as a few months."

"Will I see my father?"

"Yes."

A little farther on he sniffed, and Maigret pretended not to notice.

When they got back to the hotel, the Superintendent slipped a little money and the passkey into an envelope addressed to the Gilmore Hotel.

"I was going to take it off to France!"

Then, to Alain, who didn't know what to do:

"You coming?"

They took the elevator. There was a light on in Jeanne Debul's room; perhaps she was expecting a visit from Maigret. She would have to wait a long time.

"Come in! There are twin beds."

And, because his companion seemed embarrassed:

"You can go to bed in all your clothes if you prefer."

He arranged to be called at half past five, slept deeply, without a shadow of a dream. As for Alain, the telephone bell didn't wake him from his sleep.

"Time to get up!"

Did François Lagrange wake his son?

Right to the very end, it wasn't like any other case.

"Still, I'm very glad."

"About what?"

"That you didn't shoot. Let's not talk about that any more. . . ."

Pyke was waiting for them in the lobby, exactly the same as the day before, and it was another glorious morning.

"Nice day, isn't it?"

"Splendid!"

The car was at the door. Maigret realized that he had forgotten to introduce them.

"Alain Lagrange. Mr. Pyke, a friend from Scotland Yard."

Pyke made a sign that he understood, and didn't ask any questions. The whole way he talked about the flowers in his garden and the wonderful shade of the hydrangeas he had obtained after long years of experiment.

The plane took off, without a cloud in the sky, nothing but a fine morning haze.

"What are those?" the young man asked, pointing to

the paper receptacles put there for the convenience of passengers.

"In case anyone feels sick . . ."

Was it on account of this that, a few minutes later, Alain went pale, then green, and, with a despairing look, leaned over his receptacle?

He would have given so much not to be ill, especially in front of Superintendent Maigret!

9

IT HAD ALL HAPPENED as usual, except that a month had not elapsed since the last dinner; in fact, it was a good deal less. First of all, Pardon's voice on the telephone.

"Are you free tomorrow evening?"

"Probably."

"With your wife, of course."

"Yes."

"Do you like *tête de veau en tortue*?"

"Don't know it."

"Do you like calf's head?"

"Well enough."

"Then you'll like it mock turtle. It's a dish discovered on a visit to Belgium. You'll see. But, frankly, I don't know what wine to serve with it. . . . Perhaps some beer?"

At the last moment Pardon, as he explained with almost scientific precision, had decided on a light Beaujolais.

Maigret and his wife had walked there and had avoided looking at each other as they passed Rue Popincourt. Jussieu, from the Forensic Laboratory, was present, and Mme Maigret said he was a confirmed old bachelor.

"I wanted to invite Professor Journe. He said he never dines in town. It's twenty years since he had a meal outside his own home."

The windows were open, and the wrought-iron balcony traced its arabesques against a sky of deepening blue.

"Isn't it a wonderful evening?"

Maigret gave a little smile, which the others could not understand. He had two helpings of *tête de veau*. Over coffee, Pardon, who was passing cigars around, absent-mindedly handed the box to Maigret.

"No, thanks. Only at the Savoy."

"You smoked a cigar at the Savoy?" His wife was astonished.

"I had to. They came and whispered in my ear that pipes were forbidden."

Pardon had arranged the dinner solely in order to talk about the Lagrange affair, and everyone was being careful not to steer the conversation onto that topic. They talked about everything else, idly, except that one subject that was in everyone's mind.

"Did you pay a visit to Scotland Yard?"

"I didn't have time."

"How do you get on with them?"

"Excellently. They're the most tactful people in the world."

He meant it; he kept a soft spot for Mr. Pyke, who had raised his hand in farewell the moment the plane took off, and who had, perhaps, at heart, been rather touched.

"Much work at the Quai des Orfèvres just now?"

"Just the usual stuff. Much illness in the district?"

"The usual, too."

Then there was a little talk about illnesses. So that it was ten o'clock when Pardon finally made up his mind to murmur:

"Have you seen him?"

"Yes. Have you seen him, too?"

"I've been there twice."

The women, tactfully, were pretending not to listen. As for Jussieu, the affair was out of his hands, and he was looking through the window.

"Was he confronted with his son?"

"Yes."

"Did he say anything?"

Maigret shook his head.

"Same old story?"

For François Lagrange was sticking to his original attitude, curling up like a frightened animal. The moment anyone approached him he cowered against the wall, an arm crooked over his face to protect himself.

"Don't hit me.... I don't want to be hit...."

He even managed to make his teeth chatter.

"What does Journe think about it?"

This time it was Maigret who asked the question.

"Journe is a clever man, probably one of our best psychiatrists. He's also a man worried to death by his responsibilities."

"I understand."

"Furthermore, he has always been opposed to capital punishment."

Maigret made no comment, drew slowly on his pipe.

"One day, when I was talking to him about fishing, he looked at me with a shocked expression. He doesn't even kill fish."

"So that . . . ?"

"If François Lagrange keeps it up for another month . . ."

"Will he keep it up?"

"He's frightened enough to do so. Unless someone forces the issue . . ."

Pardon was staring intently at Maigret. This was the reason for the dinner, the question he had long waited to ask, which he expressed only with a look.

"As far as I am concerned," murmured the Superintendent, "it has nothing to do with me now. I have handed in my report. Rateau, the Examining Magistrate, for his part, will follow the experts."

Why did Pardon seem to be saying thank you? It was embarrassing. Maigret was a little put out with him for this indiscretion. It was true to say that it had nothing to do with him now. He could, obviously, have . . .

"I have other fish to fry." He sighed, rising to his feet. "Among others, a certain Jeanne Debul. She returned to Paris yesterday. She's still brazening it out. Within the next two months I hope to have her in my office for a cozy talk."

"Anyone would think you had a private quarrel with her," remarked Mme Maigret, although she had not seemed to be listening.

Nothing more was said about it. A quarter of an hour later, in the darkness of the street, Mme Maigret took her husband's arm.

166

"It's odd," he said. "The street lamps in London, though they're really almost the same . . ."

And, as they went along, he began to tell her about the Strand, Charing Cross, Trafalgar Square.

"I thought you hardly had time to eat."

"I went out for a few minutes in the evening after dinner."

"By yourself?"

"No. With him."

She didn't ask whom he meant. As they approached Boulevard Richard-Lenoir, he must have remembered the pub where he had drunk a glass of beer before going to bed. It made him thirsty.

"You don't mind if . . ."

"Of course not! Go and have a drink. I'll wait for you."

For it was a little bar where she would have felt in the way. When he came out, wiping his mouth, she took his arm again.

"Beautiful night."

"Yes."

"With lots of stars."

Why did the sight of a cat which, as they came by, dived into a ventilator cloud his face for a moment?

Shadow Rock Farm
Lakeville, Conn.
June 1952